"Those who do not complain
are never pitied."

Jane Austen, *Pride and Prejudice*

Who Killed A.J. Fryerson?

The Good Folks of Lennox Valley

Fall & Winter 1998

by Kevin Slimp

Market
Square
BOOKS

©2020 Market Square Publishing, LLC.
Knoxville, Tennessee

Who Killed A.J. Fryerson?

The Good Folks of Lennox Valley

Fall & Winter 1998

©2020 Kevin Slimp
books@marketsquarebooks.com
P.O. Box 23664   Knoxville, Tennessee 37933

ISBN13: 978-1-950899-16-6
Library of Congress: 2020946456

Printed and Bound in the United States of America

Cover Illustration ©2020 Market Square Publishing, LLC
by Danny Wilson
(dannywilson.com)

Author: Kevin Slimp
Executive Editor: Kristin Lighter
Editors: Cathy Sloan and Jean Henderson
Creative Assistant: Earl Goodman

Table of Contents

Preface 1

A.J. Fryerson 3

A.J.'s Enemies 5

Foul Play?. 7

Who Killed A.J.?. 9

Marvin & Maxine's Rumor Mill . . . 13

Heated Rivals 17

He's Back!. 21

Strike Two! 25

News War 29

Rumor Has It 33

Fighting Back 37

Biblically Speaking 41

Something's Up 45

The Plot Thickens. 49

Deadline Games 53

Peculiar Habits 57

Frank's Place. 61

Ulterior Motive 65

The Barber Knows 69

Maxine's Problem. 73

Valley Constable. 77

We've Got Trouble 81

Sign of the Times 85

Silver Tongue 89

Tempers Flare. 93

Marvin and Raymond 97

Somethin's Cookin' 101

Mystery Letter 105

Marvin Silenced! 109

Stirring Up the Church 113

What's Going On?. 117

Iris's Instincts. 121

Deacon Digging. 125

Hair-Raising 129

Iris Has Gone Too Far 133

Too Funny!. 137

Marvin is Mad!. 141

Friday the 13th 145

How Dare They? 149

Breakfast with A.J. 153

Battle of the Sexes. 157

Farley's List. 161

Sarah's Secret 165

Iris Long is Up to Something 169

The Plot Thickens. 173

The "Real" Truth 177

Tongue Twisted 181

Dueling Publishers! 185

Could She Know? 189

New Year's Eve 193

Preface

In 2009, I began writing about folks I have met throughout my life. I placed them together in my hometown of Lennox Valley.

I can still hear Marvin laughing at the domino table and Elbert Lee pitching a fit because I jokingly accused him of cheating for the hundredth time during a game.

In 2015, I began rewriting the story and released it as a syndicated column in hundreds of newspapers across America. Millions of readers join me each week, enjoying my memories.

In late 2017, Market Square Books published *The Good Folks of Lennox Valley: Spring & Summer 1998*. Readers followed the exploits of Raymond Cooper, Iris Long, Brother Billy and Rev. Sarah Hyden-Smith. Soon after, readers starting asking, "When will the next *Lennox Valley* book be available?"

As in the first volume, most of the characters in *Who Killed A.J. Fryerson* are based on people I've actually known through the years. Yes, I knew an A.J. who always seemed to be complaining about something. Yes, Iris Long is still a dear friend. . .and my favorite newspaper editor. Brother Jacob still preaches shoe-less, and I still run into Mary Ann at the grocery store now and then.

At the risk of leaving a few names out, I'd like to thank a few folks who were instrumental in the completion of this book:

- My kids, Ashley and Zachary, read each chapter as it was written, laughing most of the time and inspiring me to write the next chapter. Some of my favorite memories are listening to them laugh at the dinner table as we read the exploits of Raymond Cooper and Iris Long together.

- Earl Goodman, who read each installment, offering encouragement and advice, as well as taking on the position of mailman in Lennox Valley.

- Cathy Sloan and Jean Henderson, who were editors of the original Lennox Valley columns and were instrumental in editing the original book. This was before I began my association with Market Square Books.

- Kristin Lighter, senior editor at Market Square Books and good friend.

- Iris Long, Helen Walker and Jessie Gouge, all inspirations for the Lennox Valley story.

Finally, I'd like to thank the hundreds of newspapers who ran the original *Lennox Valley* column each week and to my readers and friends who have written words of encouragement and support along the way.

Chapter One

SEPTEMBER 1998

A.J. Fryerson

The Ultimate Complainer

If you lived in Lennox Valley during my childhood, you were familiar with A.J. Fryerson. And if you knew A.J. Fryerson, you knew one thing above all: He complained about everything.

I don't mean just a few things. I mean everything.

He complained because the Valley didn't have a traffic light. Then, when the town installed its first light on Bearden's Corner, he complained about that.

He complained because he couldn't get a beer at either of the town's eating establishments. Then, when the town held a referendum and the Hoffbrau started serving beer, he complained about that.

He complained because all the "preachers in town" were "older than dirt." Then he complained when the Lutherans called Brother Jacob, and he complained even louder when he learned the young pastor preached in his bare feet.

Simply put, A.J. lived to complain, and like most folks who complain all the time, hardly anyone noticed when A.J. got hot under the collar.

He was the most frequent caller on "Renderings with Raymond," and after Raymond took a break from airing his show following his mayoral defeat, A.J. complained about that.

Iris Long, editor of *The Hometown News*, had a love-hate relationship with A.J. On one hand, she would tell her friends A.J. was "dumber than dirt." On the other hand, Fryerson could be counted on to provide at least one letter to the editor each week. Although no one gave much, if any, thought to A.J.'s rantings, they would pick up the paper to see what he was complaining about this week.

Vera Pinrod liked to say, "A.J. Fryerson could start a fight in an empty house."

Once, after he spewed out a tirade on Raymond Cooper's show, Lori Martindale told the crowd at Caroline's Beauty Salon, "A.J. is two pickles short of a jar."

That brought a good laugh from everyone including Sylvia Snodderly, who was seldom known to crack a smile.

Sometimes A.J. would go overboard. Instead of making people laugh at how ridiculous he could be, there were times he would make folks downright angry. Like the time he had his oil changed at Floyd Phibb's Auto Service. Floyd owned one of two auto repair shops in town and was loved by everyone. Well, everyone except A.J.

In 1997, two weeks after having the oil changed in his 1991 Ford Taurus, A.J. began to notice loud squeaking in the back of his car. He ignored it for weeks until finally, while driving down the steepest hill in Lennox Valley, his brakes failed. He went off the road and ran directly into the front porch of the home of Marvin and Delores Walsh.

That was the beginning of one of A.J.'s most memorable tirades. He was convinced, and spent months letting everyone know, Floyd had overfilled the oil in his Taurus, causing it to "spill over" and spread to the back of his car, "leaking like a sieve" all over his brakes.

He threatened to sue Floyd, writing eight letters to the editor and making more than 40 calls to Raymond's show to talk about his brakes. Eventually, every lawyer in Spring County refused to take A.J.'s case.

Yes, A.J. Fryerson complained about everything. That ended, however, in late 1998, when A.J.'s complaining suddenly stopped.

Chapter Two

A.J.'s Enemies

The List Keeps Getting Longer

Yes, A.J. Fryerson complained about everything, and the number of folks on his "bad list" increased by the week. There's a funny thing about collecting such a long list. Chances are, a lot of those folks included A.J. on their bad lists as well. Sooner or later, people would say, something bad was going to happen to A.J.

The September 8, 1998 edition of *The Hometown News* included A.J.'s latest discourse. Not a week went by that Fryerson didn't write a letter to the editor, and on slow news weeks, they often found their way onto Iris Long's opinion page.

His latest rant had to do with the only gas station in town, Buford Levitt's Sinclair Oil. The problem with complaining about Levitt's was obvious to anyone in The Valley. Along with Perry Pratt, Buford was just about the most liked and respected merchant in the community. A.J. wasn't going to attract many allies.

His latest diatribe had to do with the way the gas pumps kept track of his purchases. It started when Buford introduced "self-service" pumps at his station in 1997.

Prior to that, customers would pull into the station, order their gas, and pay the attendant. More times than not, the rotating cylinder would turn over by a penny or two, but the attendant always charged only what the customer ordered.

Buford replaced his old gas pumps during the same period he introduced self-service. Instead of the old cylinder models, Levitt's now had electronic pumps with digital displays that indicated the amount of gas purchased.

This apparently upset A.J. to no end. He penned his letter on Monday, September 7, and dropped it off at the newspaper office, saving him the cost of a 32-cent stamp.

Unlike most Valley residents, Iris saw A.J.'s rantings as harmless. She figured she was doing the Valley a favor by letting him blow off steam in the paper rather than finding a more violent method of expressing himself. And sometimes, as was the case with this letter, she found A.J.'s thought process rather amusing.

"Dear Hometown News," he began. "I have been a customer of Sinclair Oil for more than 30 years. When I purchased my first car in 1963, I bought my first tank of gas from Buford Levitt himself."

Like many of A.J.'s letters, this one started out peacefully enough. But as was often the case, his tone quickly changed.

"What I want to know is," he continued, "when did gas pumps go from calculating the cost of your gas to robbing you like a slot machine in Las Vegas?"

The crux of the matter came down to the precision of those new pumps.

"Before Sinclair got those new pumps, you knew what your gas was going to cost. Now, you might as well close your eyes, because those numbers keep on rolling until they decide to stop on their own!"

He went on to call Buford the worst kind of thief: one who would steal from his neighbors and friends.

Yes, A.J. Fryerson made a lot of enemies, and as his list got longer many folks figured it was only a matter of time before he complained about someone who wouldn't take it as calmly as Buford Levitt.

The letter to the editor on September 8 would be the last anyone would hear from A.J. in 1998. Yes, he liked to complain. But as the good folks of Lennox Valley would soon discover, A.J. had just complained for the last time.

Chapter Three

Foul Play?

A.J.'s Disappearance Raises Questions in The Valley

A week had gone by since A.J. Fryerson's letter to the editor concerning Buford Levitt's new gas pumps was published in *The Hometown News*. Iris Long, editor, thought it peculiar she hadn't received anything from A.J. in the week since.

A.J. could be counted on for at least one, and sometimes two or three, submissions each week. She didn't always include a letter from A.J. on the opinion page, but Iris couldn't remember a week since his memorable letter of August 2, 1991, that she hadn't received at least one dispatch from the town complainer.

In that missive, A.J. was angry with the Valley's sole law enforcer, Chief Dibble. It seems during his first month as chief, Dibble stopped Fryerson for failure to come to a complete stop at Bearden's Corner. This was before the town's only red light was installed, and the four-way stop kept drivers from crashing into each other in front of the Baptist church.

A.J. was full of himself that day, writing, "Perhaps Chief Dibble was so focused on his chocolate donut that he failed to realize I stopped for a full seven seconds before turning right at the corner."

"The law," he continued, "requires just three seconds before making that turn."

Fryerson was confident of the timing because he remembered singing the classic line from the 1980's hit, "Come On Eileen," while he waited to make his turn.

No one living in The Valley at the time has forgotten the crescendo of his classic letter: "I have listened to 'Come On Eileen'

7

23 times this morning, and I can write with certainty the line lasts a full seven seconds."

He went on to make several additional comments about the chief's eating habits and suggested an appropriate nickname for Dibble might be "Chief Dribble," resulting from "all the chocolate dripping down his chin."

No one is sure what, if anything, Chief Dibble said or did in response to Fryerson's tirade, but it was six weeks before A.J. submitted his next letter, and he hasn't written a negative word about our beloved police chief since.

Iris had lunch at the Hoffbrau that day, taking the opportunity to ask her waitress and friend, Jessie Orr, if she had seen much of Fryerson over the past week. It was common knowledge A.J. was a daily customer at the 'Brau. Long couldn't begin to remember the number of letters he had written complaining about something that "just didn't taste right" during one of his meals.

"I haven't seen A.J. since last Wednesday," Jessie answered. "It was right after I read his letter in the paper. I told him no one was gonna side with him against Buford Levitt."

"And you haven't seen him since?" queried Iris.

"I figured he was sick or something," offered Jessie. "I can't remember the last time he missed two days in a row."

"Maybe he is," Long responded.

Iris was a veteran journalist, and she wasn't about to create unnecessary drama. After all, A.J. could be sick. Or maybe he took a trip, as unlikely as that seemed.

As she finished drinking the last sip of her coffee, Iris thought about the many enemies Fryerson had made over the years.

Even so, she could not have realized A.J. had submitted his last letter of 1998 to *The Hometown News*.

Chapter Four

SEPTEMBER 1998

Who Killed A.J.?

Valley Residents Want to Know

Three weeks had passed and still no one had seen or heard a peep from A.J. Fryerson. Something was amiss and the good folks of the Valley were starting to wonder what had happened to the town complainer.

Jessie, waitress at the Hoffbrau, taped a black and white photo of A.J. from a 1995 edition of *The Hometown News* on the side of a milk carton, resembling the photos of missing children found on cartons from the local dairy. She placed it next to the register, which initiated comments from most customers as she rang up their orders.

"I knew this was bound to happen someday," quipped Marvin Walsh. "A.J. just never knows when to keep quiet."

It was funny hearing Walsh, possibly the town's third biggest loudmouth, behind Raymond Cooper and A.J. Fryerson, call someone else out for talking too much.

"I'll bet it was Chief Dibble," Marvin said to anyone within earshot. "He can be one mean fellow."

Maxine Miller, writer of "Rumor Has It" each week in *The Hometown News*, was all ears. She scribbled copious notes of everything she heard.

When Marvin realized Maxine was in the room, he quickly changed his temperament. "Of course, I was just joking about the Chief. He's a fine law officer and he will get to the bottom of this."

For once, Walsh wished he had kept his big mouth shut.

"I think it was Buford Levitt," mumbled Earl Goodman, Valley

9

postman and respected citizen. As the only "federal official" in The Valley, Earl's opinion carried a lot of weight. "You saw what A.J. wrote about him three weeks ago."

The general consensus in the room was, as offended as he surely had to have been, Buford didn't have a violent bone in his body. It had to be someone else.

At that moment, Iris Long entered the diner for her morning coffee. Iris wasn't wrong very often, but if she thought she was going to have a quiet moment to begin her morning, she had miscalculated the sudden interest in A.J.

"You're the reporter," shouted Elbert Lee Jones. "What do you think has happened to A.J.?"

Sipping her coffee, then placing the cup on the table in front of her, Iris responded. "I don't know. None of us knows. Perhaps he took a vacation."

"I saw his silver Taurus in front of his house when I delivered his mail yesterday," shouted Goodman. "How could he take a vacation without his car?"

Jessie spoke up, which was unusual for her. "Has he been getting his mail?"

"As a federal official, I am under oath to keep matters related to an individual's mail secret," Earl spoke proudly. "However, I can say that I've been getting a good workout trying to stuff mail into full boxes lately."

Earl sat up on his stool, quite proud of himself for so deftly keeping his promise.

"Has anyone been in his house?" asked Jessie. "Do we know for sure he's not in there?"

Iris spoke up. "Chief Dibble has called a press conference for 10:00 this morning. I will be there and will report all the pertinent information in tomorrow's paper."

The veteran newspaper editor knew something wasn't right.

While she publicly stated A.J. could be on a trip or have another reason for his absence, she had known A.J. Fryerson for too long to think he would slip off silently.

As she rubbed her cup, she wondered if she should tell her fellow diners about the recent letter from A.J. she didn't print. She quickly realized this was not the right time.

That seemed to settle the room for the moment as Long seemed to again focus on her coffee. Coffee, however, was the last thing on her mind at the moment.

Chapter Five

Marvin & Maxine's Rumor Mill

Fueled by A.J.'s Disappearance

As was usually the case in late September, leaves and temperatures were falling as the Good Folks of Lennox Valley woke on Wednesday morning. In a small town like ours, it was common to rise earlier than most of the residents in Springfield, 11 miles away. We had more than our share of farmers and folks who grew up on farms, so waking up early was just part of our DNA.

A lot of folks missed hearing Raymond Cooper's voice welcome them at "sign on" each morning on Talk Radio 88.3. The station still played "God Bless The USA," but with the election four weeks past, Cooper still hadn't returned to the air.

The station carried mostly syndicated programming to fill the void. Valley residents were getting their fill of information about UFO sightings in England, political conspiracy theories and radio preachers. In an effort to appease his loyal listeners, Raymond asked Marvin Walsh to host "Renderings with Raymond" each afternoon until his return. Wednesday would mark Marvin's first appearance as host of the show.

Wednesday mornings were special in our town. That's when *The Hometown News* came out each week. You would think as small as our town was, everyone would already know any news before it came out in the local paper. Whether they did or not, the Valley depended on Iris Long, editor, to give them the facts each week and she held their faith as a sacred trust. Sure, there was the usual bickering about slanted reporting during the mayoral election but that was history and just about everyone in The Valley woke up on Wednesday morning hoping to learn something new about A.J.

Fryerson's disappearance.

Iris went back and forth at least a dozen times before settling on a headline. She had been a reporter and editor for longer than most Valley residents could remember and she felt the newspaper should report the news, not create it. After much deliberation, she settled on:

Press Conference Breeds More
Questions Than Answers

In essence, she described the eight-minute conference from beginning to end. There were three persons present: Chief Dibble, Iris Long, and the newest member of the press, Marvin Walsh. She didn't mention it in her story but Iris couldn't help but note how excited Walsh was about being allowed into the conference.

Apparently, A.J.'s disappearance wasn't big news in Springfield and it was obvious Chief Dibble was disappointed in the turnout.

The facts were straightforward. No one had seen Fryerson in three weeks. Dibble had obtained a warrant to search the home. Nothing was out of order. A.J. was not present but his car was in the driveway. Nothing seemed out of place or unusual in the home. There were no signs of foul play.

When it came time for questions, Long asked if the chief had contacted any friends or family. So far, Dibble had been unable to locate any friends or family of Fryerson. He seemed to be a loner.

Knowing the history between Dibble and A.J., Marvin asked, "Did you kill him, Chief?"

At that point, Iris was afraid she was going to have to break up a fight. Thankfully, cooler heads prevailed.

"No," Dibble responded, "I did not."

Maxine Miller did not need a press conference to fill her popular column, "Rumor Has It," with less inhibited observations about Marvin's publicly announced suspicions.

"Rumor has it," she began, "Marvin Walsh caused quite the commotion at the Hoffbrau on Tuesday when he named Chief Dibble his lead suspect in the disappearance of A.J. Fryerson."

Maxine loved to stir things up, and Iris had learned long ago readers expected a well-stirred pot.

Long could only imagine what Walsh would have to say on his show at noon but with all she knew about Marvin, she wasn't surprised by his opening words, "I smell a cover up!"

Iris felt it best to keep her final letter from A.J. to herself for the moment. There was no telling what might happen if word of its contents got out.

Chapter Six

Heated Rivals

Earthquake or Evil Plot? No One is Sure.

While questions surrounding the whereabouts of A.J. Fryerson dominated conversation in The Valley, the routine of daily life forged ahead. With no election or fire-breathing radio host to supply fodder for the town's rumor mill, cooler temperatures served as a reminder summer was past and, hopefully, a calming breeze would soon take its place.

Autumn traditions were plentiful in The Valley. As the ladies of the Auburn Hat Society busily made plans for the upcoming fall festival, anticipation surrounding the impending weekly bowling league added to the excitement of the season.

Our small town didn't have a lot of opportunity to excel in the arena of athletics. Ever since Valley High merged with West Central to form Central Valley High School, there's not been a lot to root for in my hometown. Sure, we had our elementary school kickball team and the church softball league, but no sporting event brought as much excitement as fall bowling.

The adults never wanted to answer our questions about it, but every teenager in The Valley had heard rumors concerning the huge fight that took place years earlier at a league game between the Valley King Pins and the Pleasant Hill Strike Force.

The story took on epic form over time. As did other groups of local youth, my friends and I would share each tidbit we could piece together concerning "The Legend of King Pin Alley." There were many different versions of the story, each attempting to one-up the others. Some included wacky stories of UFOs, knife fights or an

17

earthquake. All included some narrative where Elbert Lee Jones, a couple of decades younger and sprier, had heated words with at least two members of the Strike Force squad.

My group of friends stuck with what we knew for certain. There was a game between the two teams. Whether caused by an earthquake, as some believed, a wind blowing through a back door or some other natural cause, the game-winning pin fell to the floor in a mysterious manner, giving Pleasant Hill the victory and Elbert Lee more than he could take.

Jones, convinced some "home-cooked shenanigans" were to blame, responded in a way none of our parents would share with their innocent children. It was years later before I knew the real story behind the legend.

While Marvin Walsh served as guest host of "Renderings with Raymond" (he continued to use the show's original name in honor of his fallen comrade) on Thursday, he reminded his listeners the Pleasant Hill "Strut Force," as he liked to call them, would be facing the King Pins on Saturday at 6 p.m.

It would be the first meeting between the two teams, he reminded his listeners, since the "incident" 20 years earlier. That was as much as he had to say about the legend.

As the Auburn Hat Society met to finalize plans for the festival, just two weeks away, they listened while Marvin urged loyal citizens to make their way to Valley Lanes to watch our beloved King Pins take on the Strike Force in the two center lanes. The remaining two lanes, he reminded listeners, would be shut down during the contest.

Helen Walker was the first to speak up concerning the upcoming bowling match.

"I wonder," she said in her gentle voice, "who will take A.J.'s place on the team."

"Well, Earl thinks," Rhonda Goodman chimed in, "A.J. is hiding and will show up as a last-minute surprise just before the game begins."

"Heavens," whispered Vera Pinrod, just loud enough for everyone to hear. "That's a lot of trouble just to suprise the other team."

"Yes," answered Rhonda, "but remember what happened last time."

It was agreed to turn off the radio and discuss other matters.

"I think we all agree that the 'turned cider' incident should never happen again," Vera said loudly.

"I suppose," answered Becky Jane Geary, "but it sure livened up the bobbing for apples."

As Vera discussed cider and Marvin railed against the conniving Strike Force, Iris Long sipped coffee alone at the Hoffbrau.

Filling Iris's cup, Jessie asked, "What do you think happened to A.J.?"

"I wish I knew," answered Iris. "I really wish I knew."

Chapter Seven

SEPTEMBER 1998

He's Back!

Finally, a break in the A.J. Fryerson case

Marvin Walsh had been hosting "Renderings with Raymond" for five weeks and the stress of manning the town's only local talk show was becoming apparent. With Raymond away, the show was quickly becoming almost unbearable. Each day at 12:13 p.m., the first caller would be Leon Willis.

"Marvin, when is Raymond coming back?" Leon would whine into the phone.

For the first couple of weeks, Marvin did his best to assure Leon, as well as other listeners, Cooper was doing just fine. He was recuperating from the pressures of managing the Valley's "only real news center" while running for mayor at the same time.

"Raymond Cooper refuses to give you, his loyal fans, anything other than his absolute best!" Walsh would almost yell into the microphone.

Additionally, Marvin had a farm to tend to, and not just any farm. Walsh's farm was the second biggest in the county, and even with farmhands it was a full-time job to keep cows milked and egg baskets filled.

This Friday's show would be different, however. It began as usual with Lee Greenwood singing, "God Bless the USA." During a quick recap of local news, Valley residents were told there were "no new breaks" in the A.J. Fryerson story.

There was something different in Marvin's voice, however. He sounded peppier. The pace of his reading and the pitch of his voice had increased from previous shows. That's when Marvin shared the "breaking news" with his listeners.

"I won't be taking calls during the first hour of our show today," Walsh explained. "We have a very special guest with us."

Kelly Schmidt and the rest of the customers at Caroline's Beauty Salon quickly tried to guess who the special guest would be.

"I'll bet it's Silver Tongue," Kelly speculated.

Vera was quick to put a damper on that notion. "Why would he have Dick Bland on the show after the way he talked about him during the election?"

Kelly agreed.

"I'll just bet it's Sheriff Dibble," shouted Rhonda Goodman. "Maybe he's going to tell us what happened to A.J."

Following a quick commercial for Farley Puckett's True Value Hardware Store, Marvin was back and the salon hushed in silence.

Marvin was so excited, he sounded like a kid trying to hold in a high guarded secret.

"There's no need to keep you in suspense any longer," Walsh told his listeners. "I have none other than our champion, Raymond Cooper, with me on the show."

You could almost hear a collective gasp as folks throughout the Valley took in the news.

"Let's get right to it, Mayor ... I mean, Raymond. What do you have to tell your fans?"

"First, let me say how wonderful it is to be behind this microphone again," Raymond said in a hushed voice. "I could feel the prayers and supplications of all my listeners rising up to heaven while I've been away."

After a dramatic pause, he continued. "I have two important announcements I would like to share with our listeners today."

"Oh my, he's dying!" shouted Kelly.

"I'll bet he was away solving the A.J. Fryerson case," Rhonda shot back.

"I am greatly chagrined at the lack of progress in the biggest missing person investigation in Valley history," Raymond said, "and I believe much of the fault lies with our so-called newspaper editor who, instead of investigating any leads to bring this case to light, has taken valuable time from our chief, forcing him to hold press conferences and interviews so she can have fodder for her supermarket tabloid.

"In response," he continued, "as a God-fearing and loyal citizen, I have decided to start a real newspaper called *The Valley Patriot*."

"Heavens to Betsy," gasped Marvin. "What's your other announcement?"

"I have agreed to take A.J. Fryerson's place as captain of the Valley King Pins in their match against the Pleasant Hill Strike Force tomorrow night at Valley Lanes."

"Wow!" shouted Earl Goodman to no one in particular as he listened on his postal jeep radio. "This is great!"

At that very moment, Sarah Hyden-Smith, pastor of the Methodist church, took a sip of coffee as she finished lunch at the Hoffbrau.

"Good Lord," murmured Jessie as she warmed up Sarah's coffee.

"Don't blame him," Sarah responded.

Hundreds of newspapers throughout the United States and Canada ran weekly installments of *The Good Folks of Lennox Valley* each week. Some, like *The Paper of Montgomery County* (Indiana), ran the column on the front page.

Chapter Eight

Strike Two!

Pandemonium reigns in Valley grudge match

It has been 18 years since the unforgettable match between the Valley King Pins and the Pleasant Hill Strike Force, and for the life of me I still can't figure out how they fit 237 fans, plus several infants, into that four-lane bowling alley.

I was one of the lucky ones. Mary Ann Tinkersley and I were on our third "official" date that night, and like many others, we were rife with anticipation. My plan had been to buy two chili dogs, chips and sodas before the first game, but the line at the concession stand made that an impossibility.

Chester Fleenor, Valley Lanes owner, had anticipated a big crowd, but he never dreamed nearly 200 good folks of the Valley would show up, in addition to more than thirty fans who came to cheer on the Strike Force. He and his daughter, Kari Lynn, manned the stand alone, leaving Chester's son, Phil, to oversee the equipment. This was no night to have a problem with the pins or scoreboards. Too much was at stake.

There were three primary reasons for the huge turnout. First, everyone in The Valley had heard the story of Elbert Lee Jones taking on the entire foursome of Strike Force behemoths in an act of sheer bravery and loyalty to his home town. Even though it had been 20 years, the wounds were still fresh.

Second, Raymond Cooper's return to anchor the bowling team brought out many of his loyal fans, eager to see their champion single-handedly run the evildoers from Pleasant Hill straight back from where they came. To the Valley faithful, the Strike Force team was anything but pleasant.

Third, there were those who thought A.J. Fryerson might show up. He was normally the anchor of the King Pins and if he was alive, he would surely make his way to Valley Lanes to lead his team to victory.

As the giant clock directly above the dividing line between lanes 2 and 3 struck 7 o'clock, it was clear to everyone A.J. wouldn't be defending the honor of our town. There was an almost deafening roar as the Lennox Valley squad was introduced.

Earl Goodman was the first to wave to the crowd as his name was called and he would be the first to roll for the King Pins. Next was Perry Pratt, owner of Valley General Store. In years past, Marvin Walsh would have been the third bowler introduced, but after his 65th birthday he turned the duties over to Billy Joe Drury. Billy Joe kept to himself mostly and was a bit gruff for someone who grew up in The Valley, but he was a good bowler and the fans cheered as he painstakingly raised his hand just above his waist.

The loudest cheers of the night were reserved for Raymond Cooper, wearing his orange-striped yellow shirt, which happened to be the school colors of the defunct Lennox Valley High School, along with an "awe shucks" smile while soaking in the adulation.

The crowd grew silent as Earl Goodman rolled the first ball, a "flat ten." In bowling lingo, that is a ball which knocks down all but the ten pin, leaving the six pin lying in the gutter. It felt as if the entire Valley cheering squad breathed a sigh of relief.

The first bowler for Pleasant Hill rolled a "flush," meaning all ten pins landed in the pit. Any experienced bowler knows a flush strike is technically perfect. The Strike Force loyals cheered in anticipation of a sweeping victory.

What happened next is second-hand information. The line to the concession stand had finally shortened to three deep and I made my way to buy those chili dogs and sodas. Just as I was handing $3 to Mr. Fleenor, I heard a deafening roar. I turned to look, but everyone in the crowd was standing and yelling, keeping me from seeing what was happening.

The commotion continued for what seemed like several minutes, but probably lasted no more than 15 or 20 seconds. By the time I made my way close enough to see what was transpiring, Billy Joe was lying flat on the ground and emotions ranged from concern for Billy's safety, to jubilation among the Pleasant Hill crowd who sensed a forfeit, to bewilderment among the remaining King Pins.

Harsh words were being exchanged between the two teams but the roar of the crowd drowned them out. Finally, the Strike Force gathered their equipment and walked out to a chorus of boos from Lennox supporters.

Raymond made his way to the concession stand, taking Mr. Fleenor's microphone in his hand.

"Be sure," Raymond said, "to pick up a copy of *The Lennox Valley Patriot* this Tuesday for a full report of what just transpired."

Iris Long, still in her seat just behind lane 4, dropped her reporter's pad, briefly stunned.

"Tuesday," she whispered to herself, "One day before *The Hometown News.*"

27

Chapter Nine

News War

Cooper throws gauntlet at Hometown News

Iris Long hadn't slept much since Saturday night's bowling match, where Raymond Cooper made the announcement concerning the first issue of his competing newspaper, *The Valley Patriot,* premiering Tuesday morning. Iris knew Raymond "like the back of her hand," and she was certain he was repaying her for supporting his opponent in the recent mayoral campaign.

Two days later, on Monday morning, Cooper not only appeared as the newest publisher in town after a six-week absence, but also returned to his seat behind the microphone at Talk Radio 88.3, just in time to promote "the Valley's new home for honest news." Raymond told his listeners "their" newspaper could be picked up at several locations throughout The Valley including Farley Puckett's True Value, Pratt's General Store and, of course, in front of Talk Radio 88.3 on Main Street.

Raymond didn't give any clues about the contents of his new paper, other than to remind listeners it would include the news they wanted to read, not topics "forced down their throats like nasty medicine," obviously referring to *The Hometown News.*

Sitting in a booth at the Hoffbrau on Tuesday, Iris sipped coffee across from Juliette Stoughton. She could only imagine what *The Patriot* would include.

"I wonder what time it will come out," Juliette pondered aloud.

"All he said was Tuesday morning," her friend responded.

Iris was obviously worried. She confided in Juliette she had already lost three advertisers to Raymond's paper.

"Apparently," she told Juliette, "he's almost giving ads away to anyone who agrees to move their accounts from *The Hometown News* to his rag."

"There's got to be something we can do," offered Juliette. "He can't get away with this. You know he's just trying to get back at you after losing the election."

Their conversation was interrupted when Sarah Hyden-Smith, pastor at Lennox Valley Methodist Church, came rushing in.

"They're out," Sarah said in a nervous tone. She was carrying two copies of the paper. "I haven't looked. I waited so we could look at it together."

Sarah, Juliette and Iris had become close friends during the recent mayoral campaign. It was Juliette who dropped out of the campaign, clearing the path for "Silver Tongue" Dick Bland to win re-election. Anything was better, she believed, than seeing Raymond Cooper as mayor. It never dawned on her, or anyone else, Raymond would create a competing newspaper.

Sarah handed both folded copies of The Patriot to Iris, who opened them on the table amid the trio as Hoffbrau waitress Jessie joined them. There was momentary silence as all four gazed at the front page.

"Bland Steals Election" was emblazoned across the front page in 80-point type. Below was a photo of Iris Long speaking with Mayor Dick Bland during the final vote count just weeks earlier. It stretched across all six columns of the front page.

Two-thirds down the page was another headline, smaller than the first but still larger than most headlines in *The Hometown News*: "Cooper Vows to Lead Search for Missing Citizen."

A Table of Contents in the bottom-right corner hinted at what would follow on the inside pages.

Valley King Pins Report . . . . *Page 2*

Opinion Page . . . . *Page 3*

Church News . . . . *Page 4*

Farley's True Value . . . . *Page 5*

Political Review . . . . *Page 6*

Raymond's Renderings . . . . *Page 6*

Classifieds . . . . *Page 7*

That's when all four readers saw it. Iris sat, speechless, as if her eyes were playing tricks on her.

"I can't believe it," she muttered.

"Is that what I think it is?" Juliette said as she looked closer.

"Holy cow!" Jessie shouted, before catching herself.

"I can't believe it," Iris whispered again. "Rumor Has It with Maxine Miller." She stopped to catch her breath before continuing, "Page 8."

Chapter Ten

SEPTEMBER 1998

Rumor Has It

Maxine Miller Can't Be Trusted

"I can't believe it," Iris whispered over and over. "I just can't believe it."

Iris noticed her most popular columnist hadn't dropped off her column by Monday as usual, but she figured Maxine was working on a last-minute scoop or some extra-juicy bit of gossip. Never in a thousand years would Iris Long imagine her long-time writer and friend betraying her like this, but there it was in black and white.

To make matters worse, Maxine's column was planted at the top of page 8, in the same location readers had become accustomed to finding her weekly feature in *The Hometown News*.

Raymond Cooper had really done it this time. First, he creates a rival publication to get back at Iris for her support of Juliette Stoughton in the mayoral race, then he plasters a picture of Iris talking with Mayor Bland on the front page under the headline, "Bland Steals Election."

Most readers would see beyond Cooper's attempt at linking Iris with Bland's victory, but for Raymond's loyal supporters, that photo was proof the election was manipulated by the elite media of the Valley.

Long often told friends there was nothing Raymond Cooper could do that would surprise her. Obviously, she never imagined he would stoop this low.

"Rumor has it," Maxine's column began, "media sources in The Valley conspired to sway the recent election."

Seated across from her friends in a Hoffbrau booth, Iris dropped the paper on the table in front of her. She seemed a bit disoriented.

Sarah Hyden-Smith quickly left her seat and moved next to her friend.

"No one will believe this trash," Sarah offered. "Everyone knows Raymond is a weasel."

"Everyone," Iris interrupted, "except half the Valley who voted for him."

Iris felt her world crashing around her. The same woman who created such memorable headlines as "Homeless Man Under House Arrest" and "City Unsure Why the Sewer Smells" was suddenly without words. In the previous 24 hours, she learned three of her regular advertisers had jumped ship and, now, the most popular columnist in *The Hometown News* had joined them.

Publications like *The Hometown News* were like small town newspapers across America. The paper was a labor of love for Iris, who knew every community needed an honest source of news. The good folks of the Valley clipped pictures of their children holding ribbons at the 6th grade spelling bee, learned what was happening at school board meetings and knew what their elected officials were up to, thanks to the hard work of Iris Long.

There would always be a few readers like A.J. Fryerson. He would complain about the biased reporting and slanted news, but A.J. complained about everything and everyone in The Valley knew it.

Iris could only imagine what would happen if she had to shut down her paper. She wasn't sure how *The Hometown News* could survive with advertisers moving to Raymond's Valley Patriot.

If Cooper was successful, he would control Valley media, owning the town's only radio station and newspaper.

"We're not going to let it happen," Juliette chimed in. "You've done too much good for too long. The people of Lennox Valley love you and *The Hometown News*."

That's when Sarah noticed a few typos.

"Jeremy Joyce admitted to hospital with third-degree buns," she read aloud with a giggle. "The buns," she continued, "came after he came in contact with a high-voltage wife."

Pretty soon everyone in the restaurant was huddled around their booth. It was soon apparent that Raymond lacked both a proofreader and an understanding of journalistic ethics.

"I wouldn't throw in the towel just yet," Hoffbrau waitress Jessie chimed in.

It wasn't long until everyone in the 'Brau was joining in the laughter.

"Look at this one!" shouted Ken Rochelle. "On page 3."

There it was, just under the "Local Events" heading:

Valley Youth Cook & Serve Grandparents

"Well, maybe it's not going to be as bad as I thought," chuckled Iris.

Chapter Eleven

SEPTEMBER 1998

Fighting Back

Against the "Only Honest News" in Town

There were more than a few folks in The Valley who felt Iris Long had it coming to her. After all, Raymond Cooper garnered 381 votes in the recent mayoral election, and a good number of those voters placed the blame for Cooper's defeat squarely on the shoulders of Long, editor of *The Hometown News*.

There was no need to deny the obvious. Seeing the first issue of Raymond's Valley Patriot was upsetting to Iris. She saw the masthead at the top of page 1 as a direct assault on her character.

"The Valley Patriot" was in type big enough to fill the width of the 12 x 21 inch newspaper. Underneath, in smaller type, were words that cut Iris to the core, "The only source of honest news in Lennox Valley."

"How could he write that?" Iris asked herself over and again.

It simply wasn't true. Long was a seasoned journalist. Other than columns on the Opinion page and the musings of Maxine Miller, her stories were checked and rechecked. Each story required multiple sources before appearing in the newspaper.

Iris thought long and hard about her response in *The Hometown News*, which came out one day after *The Valley Patriot*. It seemed as if almost every word in every story in Cooper's rag was pure fiction, the mutterings of a madman.

She had to be careful, though. If she wrote too harshly, Cooper's loyalists would see that as further proof *The Hometown News* was a biased arm of the "elite media," as Raymond often called it. Ignoring Raymond's indictments was also dangerous. No response would be

37

seen by many as an admission of guilt.

Instead, Iris chose to take the high road. Those who knew her well weren't surprised. Iris valued her integrity as much as anyone in The Valley.

"This morning," she began, "I read with great interest Raymond Cooper's latest venture, *The Valley Patriot*."

So far, so good.

She continued, "*The Hometown News* welcomes any legitimate journalistic endeavor to our town, and it is our hope *The Valley Patriot* will meet the requirements of journalistic integrity the citizens of our community have come to expect."

Reading over Cooper's rag, a full two-thirds of the pages, not counting ads, were dedicated to two topics: Mayor Bland conspiring with Iris Long to fix the mayoral election and the disappearance of A.J. Fryerson.

Raymond went on for 1,830 words about Fryerson. While not sharing any details, he led readers to believe he was close to solving the missing person case. There were a few leads yet to be investigated. He insinuated Chief Dibble was keeping information from the public. As a "responsible journalist," he was hard at work bringing the truth to light.

Cooper included a full page, brought to the readers by Farley Puckett's True Value Hardware Store, with a recap of the weekend bowling match between Lennox Valley and Pleasant Hill. Raymond considered it a pure stroke of genius to place a line of text in large type across the top of each page, giving credit to the page's sponsor.

The obituaries were "Brought to you in loving memory of the dear departed by Massengale's Mortuary," the funeral home located in the county seat of Springfield.

Another page was reserved for "Raymond's Renderings," sponsored by "Phil Moore's Tractors and Equipment, located midway between the Valley and Springfield."

Iris could have instantly made Cooper seem foolish by sharing information from the last letter she received from A.J. Fryerson before his disappearance. She knew, however, while offering momentary satisfaction, it was best to keep the letter to herself. In Lennox Valley, things could get quickly out of hand.

There was also the matter of filling the space reserved for "Rumor Has It." Iris was tempted to create her own rumors about Raymond Cooper, but her better judgment wouldn't allow such a breach.

She looked over *The Valley Patriot* one last time before finishing up her paper. One headline, while funny, seemed to sum up Cooper's efforts at "quality journalism."

On page 7, just above the classified section, was the headline:

Death is Nation's Top Killer

Iris, borrowing a favorite phrase from Jessie at the Hoffbrau, muttered, "Good Lord."

Chapter Twelve

OCTOBER 1998

Biblically Speaking

Raymond and Friends Share Scriptural Wisdom

Raymond Cooper was quickly learning running a newspaper took a lot more time than running a broadcast operation. With the radio station, he could flip on a couple of switches at sunrise each day and "Turn Your Radio On" would fill the airwaves. Within minutes, recorded programming would fill the airwaves until "Renderings with Raymond" went on the air at noon.

Just down the road in Springfield, deejays were preparing for "morning drive time," the busiest hours of the day. They were hurriedly preparing news bulletins, weather advisories, and light comedy routines to cheer up their early morning audience.

Most days, Raymond left for breakfast about 15 minutes after flipping the last switch. During those 15 minutes, he was listening to the drive time broadcast of FM 95.7 in Springfield, getting the news and weather forecast to share with his listeners later in the morning.

Radio stations in small towns like ours were interesting places. Before radio gave way to streaming audio on the World Wide Web, stations were hubs of activity. Raymond liked to refer to his station, Talk 880, as "500 Watts of Valley Power."

Hearing him say those words brought chills down the spines of many Valley residents. We were proud to have such capacity to influence the world right there in our own community.

I suppose that changed for me one morning while drying my hair. I noticed a number on the handle of my blow dryer that said, "1200 Watts."

It was hard to imagine my blow dryer held more horsepower

41

than Raymond's station. Truth be told, my hair dryer probably produced just as much reliable information as Talk 880, but not as much hot air.

Cooper quickly learned he wasn't going to make a profit from his new journalistic endeavour. The initial edition was hailed by his fans. Most believed it was only a short matter of time before Raymond received his first Pulitzer Prize and *The Hometown News* was relegated to history books.

A major problem for Raymond's paper was advertising. He had given most of the ads away to his friends to fill space. Farley Puckett sponsored the sports page, filled with news about the "Bowling match of the century" between Lennox Valley and Pleasant Hill, for free.

Those who did pay for ads paid very little. The first issue included three long-time advertisers from *The Hometown News*. In exchange for agreeing to stop advertising in Iris Long's "rag," they paid one-third the amount they paid previously.

Somebody had to write the news. Raymond spent weeks creating the dribble filling the pages of his first issue while he took time away from his radio duties. Now he was back on air, something had to give.

Raymond quickly recruited his best friends to help write stories for the paper and co-host his daily radio show. This made for some interesting banter. Somehow, the Thursday topic steered toward "favorite Bible verses." Callers seemed to love the topic.

"What's your favorite Bible verse?" a caller asked Marvin Walsh, who was manning the microphone.

Marvin paused for a moment to ponder his response.

"I believe," he murmured, "it would have to be either 'The Lord helps those who help themselves' or 'Everything happens for a reason.'"

Listening to the broadcast over lunch at the Hauffbrau, Brother Jacob, associate pastor at the Lutheran church, barely escaped spitting his coffee across the booth onto Sarah Hyden-Smith.

"Good Lord," Jessie, their waitress, exclaimed. "Even I know those aren't in the Bible and I haven't been to a church in 20 years."

Back at the station, Marvin and his co-host, Raymond, smugly admired their scriptural prowess as well as broadcast skills.

"What about you, Raymond?" asked Marvin. "What's yours?"

Cooper, realizing the spiritual influence he held over his listeners, gave serious thought to his response.

"I believe" he answered, "it would have to be 'What comes around, goes around.'"

"Oh, that's a good one!" Marvin shouted. "I don't know why I didn't think of that one."

Chapter Thirteen

OCTOBER 1998

Something's Up

Raymond Cooper Just Isn't Himself Lately

Still just one week into his new career as newspaper publisher, Raymond Cooper was already feeling the weight of responsibility pressing on his shoulders. In the two months since his defeat in the mayoral runoff election, it was obvious some things had changed. Taken individually, they probably wouldn't arouse suspicion, but together they provided overwhelming evidence something was up with Raymond.

Pastor Jacob was probably the first to notice Raymond's absence from the 8:30 a.m. contemporary service at Lennox Valley Lutheran Church. With an average attendance of 12, it was obvious when someone was missing.

Near the beginning of his mayoral campaign, Raymond joined the church with the fervor of a new convert at the Jordan River. No one in attendance that day will ever forget his sprint to the front of the fellowship hall, home of the early morning service. Recalling his only previous religious experience as a 5-year-old attending Pentecostal services with his grandmother, Cooper flung himself to the floor, overcome with a spiritual awaking not seen since John Wesley felt strangely warmed at Aldersgate.

Since the election, however, Raymond hadn't been seen at the contemporary service or any other event at the Lutheran church. Following such a dramatic conversion, it seemed strange for him to drop out of sight.

Listeners also noticed the absence of the daily prayers Raymond so skillfully offered on his show. Of course, they had no idea he was taking the prayers, word for word, from his copy of *Book of Famous Prayers.*

Heather Brooks, administrative assistant for the Federal Reserve's offices in Washington, noticed a significant decrease in the number of letters arriving from the good folks of Lennox Valley. The mail room at 20th Street and Constitution Avenue was a bit less hectic than it had been just a few months earlier.

For two years, up to the election, Raymond spent hours each day bemoaning the state of the Federal Reserve, and his listeners responded by sending dozens of hand-written letters each day to their offices in Washington. Since the election, it seems as if Raymond and his listeners had forgotten all about the evils of the Federal Reserve.

After a six-week absence, his fans were just thrilled to have their "champion of the airwaves" back. Most didn't notice or care about changes in Raymond's demeanor since the tragic events of late August.

When one did notice, as happened one Wednesday in mid-October when Helen Ashenfelter called the show asking Cooper where he had been on Sundays, Raymond proved adept at navigating the precarious situation.

"Thank you for your concern, Helen," he answered. Turning to Marvin Walsh, seated next to him in the broadcast booth, he said, "Marvin and I have had much conversation concerning the changes which come with public service."

"That's right," echoed Marvin, "We sure have."

"You may have read in a newspaper or seen on the TV news presidents and other officials sometimes are forced to stay away from public worship services and other events to keep the Lord's House from turning into a media circus.

"As much as I'd love to be in my house of worship on Sunday mornings," he continued, "I've chosen to keep my worship private, for the sake of the people."

Raymond's last call of the day came from Beatrice Justice. You may remember Beatrice had a peculiar custom of speaking only in Bible verses. No one living in The Valley at the time will ever forget the incident when Cooper made a snide remark concerning Beatrice's habit.

The following week, a letter to the editor, penned by Ms. Justice, was limited to the words, "Numbers 22, Verse 29."

By the time Raymond learned who was on the phone, it was too late for him to do anything to stop it.

"Yes, Ms. Justice," Marvin spoke into the microphone, "What's on your mind?"

The timid voice on the line responded, "Proverbs 19, Verse 1."

Raymond couldn't even imagine what Beatrice was talking about, but as he ended his show, more than 300 good folks in The Valley had opened their Bibles.

Chapter Fourteen

The Plot Thickens

Just When Things Were Beginning to Seem Normal

Undoubtedly, the second most popular show on Talk 880 Radio came on immediately after "Renderings with Raymond."

Raymond Cooper used to enjoy the relaxed atmosphere of "Swap Shop" after debating the issues of the day, some real and some fabricated, on his wildly popular show. Lately, however, with the burden of running the town's only radio station and publishing a weekly newspaper, Raymond found it necessary to turn the reins of "Swap Shop" over to his trusted friend, Farley Puckett.

The Friday show began with a call from a regular, as did most installments of the show.

"I've got an 80-horsepower 1963 John Deere 'four naught ten' tractor," roared the first caller, Earl Goodman, on Friday's show.

In addition to being the Valley's sole postman, Earl, like a lot of other folks in our town, raised crops on the side.

He continued, "I'd be willing to swap it for a 1984 auto-loading Browning A5 shotgun."

Like most callers to the show, Goodman knew exactly what he wanted to swap for, and who in the community had the item he desired. Sure, it might have been easier to call Elbert Lee Jones directly and offer to buy his shotgun. There was a risk, however, of enduring one of Elbert's classic tantrums, making it safer to make the offer on the air.

Thus, Earl called "Swap Shop" once or twice each week and offered to swap something for an anonymous 1984 shotgun. In four years, Jones hadn't responded to Goodman's offer, but it didn't keep

Earl from trying.

Puckett was more than Cooper's friend. He was his biggest advertiser. This made for some interesting banter on the show.

"I've got an antique table," Vera Pinrod, the next caller, began, "that I'd be willing to trade for a good riding lawn mower."

This was precisely the time when Farley took advantage of his on-air presence.

"You know, Vera," he interrupted, "it sounds to me like you should drop by the hardware store and take a look at the lawn mower sale going on right now."

After a moment of silence, he continued, "I would hate to see you part with such an important family heirloom like that table."

Little did he, or anyone else for that matter, know her table was ordered in 1976 from a Montgomery Ward catalog. There was no real sentimental value attached to it.

The next caller was Rita Tate, part-time manicurist and six-time winner of the Valley Garden Club Award at the Spring County Fair.

"I've got a deluxe tractor scoot with garden kneeler in good shape," she began. "I'd be willing to swap it for a raised bed cultivator and . . ."

That's when Farley jumped in. "You know, Mrs. Tate, it sounds like we've got just the thing for you at Puckett's Hardware. We've got a raised cultivator that will just about guarantee your seventh trip to the winners circle."

"Swap Shop" was beginning to sound a lot like an hour-long commercial for Farley's store. By the 51-minute mark, most listeners had turned their attention to something else, meaning they didn't hear the final caller of Friday's show.

"Who do we have on the line?" Puckett asked.

"Uhm, this is, uhm, Jeremy," mumbled the caller.

Farley knew just about everyone in Lennox Valley, so he assumed Jeremy must be from Springfield, where the "500 watts of

Valley power" could be heard most days.

"What have you got to swap today, Jeremy?" asked Puckett.

"I want to swap one of our 'so called public servants' for someone who's not crooked as a divining rod," the caller responded with a bit more force.

"Now wait just a doggone minute!" Farley shot back. "Are you talking about one of our Valley officials?"

"I am indeed," the mysterious caller answered.

A sudden "click" indicated Jeremy was no longer on the line.

As Puckett closed the show, reminding listeners to take advantage of the sale of tomato stakes at his store, there was a sense of uneasiness in his tone.

"I know that voice," he said to himself. "I know I've heard it before."

Just then, Marvin Walsh came storming into the studio.

"Do you know who that was?" Marvin asked.

"Jeremy somebody," answered Puckett.

"Jeez Louise, Farley! That wasn't no 'Jeremy somebody.' That was A.J. Fryerson!"

Chapter Fifteen

Deadline Games

A Favorite Valley Pastime

Looking back on my growing up years, it seems to me the folks in my hometown had an unhealthy infatuation with death. Unlike bigger cities, there weren't a lot of activities outside of school and work, so funerals became full-scale social events. However, the infatuation with death didn't end there.

Even things like cemeteries and tombstones took on a life of their own. We had three cemeteries in The Valley. Depending on where you were buried, the details of the grieving process could vary greatly.

For Baptists, chances are your final resting place was at First Baptist Cemetery, just south of the church grounds. My Baptist childhood friends used to tell stories of meeting up with ghosts as they played games near the cemetery after evening services.

The Catholics had their own cemetery. As a child, it seemed especially spooky because the statues and gravestones were much larger than those in our other cemeteries. The Virgin Mary might seem peaceful and angelic in daylight, but at night her shadows could be downright scary.

The Methodists had a small cemetery next to their church. Members liked having the cemetery there for insurance, among other reasons. Methodist churches, it seems, are combined into "conferences." These conferences have the ability to create new congregations and close churches who have dwindled in attendance numbers.

"Cemeteries," Essie Kennemer would say, "are like insurance.

They can't close a church with a cemetery. If they do, who's going to take care of it?"

Fortunately, the Lennox Valley Methodist Church wasn't in danger of closing. But as Essie would say, "It's good to know, just in case."

If you weren't a member at one of those churches, your eternal rest would probably take place at Shady Acres Cemetery, located between Lennox Valley and Springfield.

There are plenty of stories of folks who found religion as they advanced in years, simply to be sure they were buried in The Valley, and not down the road toward Springfield.

Funeral traditions varied with cemeteries, it seems. Our parents would tell us stories of "sitting up with the dead" when they were growing up. Thankfully, that tradition faded before I was born.

In my childhood years, Baptist funerals tended to be three-day affairs, with two nights of "visitation" before the actual event. As a teenager, sitting in a room full of relatives dressed up in their Sunday best for two straight nights seemed like cruel and unusual punishment. I understand the good folks at First Baptist Church have come to their senses in the years since.

Visitation wasn't the only drawn out aspect of a Baptist funeral. Brother Billy Joe Raymond seemed to know he had a captive audience at funerals and preached as if everyone was going to meet their end before tomorrow.

The Methodists and Lutherans had it easiest: One night of visitation, a 20-minute funeral service, then casseroles and cake.

It wasn't until I was an adult I realized Catholic wakes weren't nearly as scary as they sounded to a young Protestant. Usually, a priest offered a prayer, followed by friends and family sharing stories about the dear departed.

Folks gave a good bit of thought to their own funerals in The Valley. More than one Lutheran left specific instructions Brother Jacob was to wear shoes if he presided at their services.

Most Methodists had become comfortable with a female pastor after four months, but some older members sent requests to Glynn Vickers, their former pastor, asking if he could perform their funerals when the time came.

Speculating who was next was a routine conversation among many folks in The Valley. To some, it was almost a sport.

As October 1998 neared its end, most figured the odds favored Emma Woods, who was 102 years old. Not far behind was none other than A.J. Fryerson.

Marvin Walsh might be have been sure it was A.J.'s voice calling "Renderings with Raymond" on Friday, but others believed he was dreaming.

Yes, odds were Emma or A.J. was next. It wouldn't be long before we knew.

Chapter Sixteen

Peculiar Habits

The Ladies of the Auburn Hat Society

Outside church organizations, there were only three prominent civic groups in Lennox Valley during my teenage years.

The VFW post was formed in the 1920s by local veterans who served in the Spanish-American War and World War I. A focus of the group was to foster camaraderie among United States veterans of overseas conflicts.

In the 1960s, a few local citizens formed the Ruritan Club. Never quite as prominent as the VFW, the Ruritans' motto was, "To serve The Valley with fellowship, goodwill, and community service."

While both espoused civic duty, there was a third group in our community which seemed to attract more attention than either the VFW or Ruritans.

The Auburn Hat Society of Lennox Valley was made up of women, 50 years and older, who possessed qualities befitting members of such a society. One requirement of membership was to wear a bright auburn hat to each meeting.

Occasionally women younger than 50 asked to take part in Society gatherings. They were sometimes allowed to participate, as long as they wore a light orange fedora. Fedoras of such colors being difficult to find, it was rare younger women attended the meetings. Outsiders often commented the requirement was simply to keep them out of the group.

There was a reason for this. The secrets of the Auburn Hat Society were tightly guarded. Meetings took place at various places, but always in public areas. Since no outsiders were allowed in the group, only members of the Society knew what important matters were discussed. Not even husbands were privy to inside information.

To non-members, the obvious question was "Why meet in public if your meetings are secret?"

The question alone indicates they have missed the point entirely, because the real reason for the existence of the Auburn Hat Society was twofold: To be seen and to have fun being seen.

At the October meeting of the Auburn Hat Society, Vera Pinrod sported a bright auburn cowboy hat. Once awarded National Auburn Hatter of the Year, the highest honor bestowed on a member, Vera took great care to be a model president. Wanda Jones donned a tulle-trimmed affair that stood out among the group.

Before the days of Google, outsiders had few resources to learn about the Society. Little did they know the official purpose of the Auburn Hatters was to "promote periods of respite from the cares and drudgery of everyday life in which members gather for no other purpose than to play."

The October meeting was an especially celebratory affair, as the club took a "journey" to Springfield, our county seat, to feast at Red Lobster.

With only a couple of eateries in The Valley, it was quite a treat to travel 16 miles for dinner at a luxurious restaurant. Though she was normally the most vocal opponent of alcohol being served in Valley eating establishments, Vera either forgot her reservations concerning "the Devil's brew" while out of town or simply stuck by her assertion that a strawberry mojito was "nothing more than Sprite with a kick."

Official business consisted of selecting a parade queen to represent the Society in the upcoming Valley Christmas parade. Helen Walker, parade queen for the previous 11 years was nominated and selected in less than 40 seconds, leaving ample time to enjoy mojitos and traipse around the restaurant in their flamboyant headgear.

An unstated rule was each member took a "royal potty break"

at least twice during dinner to allow diners to admire their headwear and wonder what important business was being carried out in secret.

As the group left Red Lobster, Vera stopped in her tracks, watching a silver Dodge Stratus pulling out of the parking lot.

"Did anyone else see that?" she asked.

"See what?" asked Rhonda Graham.

"That car. I'm sure I saw Raymond Cooper and A.J. Fryerson in that car."

"How many 'Sprites with a kick' did you have?" bellowed Helen Walker.

The parade of Auburn Hatters roared with laughter, but Vera stood still, contemplating what she was sure she had just seen.

Chapter Seventeen

OCTOBER 1998

Frank's Place

More Than Cuts Take Place at New Shop

Probably the best thing to happen in my hometown during October 1998 was the arrival of Frank Bell. Most folks living in The Valley at the time probably wouldn't feel this way, but to teenage boys, Frank was a godsend.

If you grew up in a big city – any place with a population greater than 3,000 – you probably wouldn't understand the complexities of being a 16-year-old boy in a place like Lennox Valley. There was literally nothing to do most of the time.

Since many of us lived on farms, we had our chores and we had school. But since Lennox Valley High School merged with West High in Springfield to form West Valley High School, extracurricular activities were kept to a minimum. It was an 11-mile drive and most of us didn't want to use up our gas by taking extra trips back and forth from the school.

Those of us on farms woke up early to do chores. Once the school year began, most of our parents let up on afternoon chores so we could enjoy an hour or two of free time after classes. Our problem was obvious. There was nothing to do. That changed when Frank Bell moved to town in October.

Frank came to The Valley from the big city, Terra Haute, Indiana. There, he was the third ranking barber in a three-chair shop. He saved his money, knowing the day would come when he would leave to start his own business.

That day came in August as he read a story in *American Barber Magazine* titled, "Towns Without Barbers." Apparently Lennox

Valley was featured, along with a dozen or so other places, as a town with no barbershop. "True," the writer mentioned, "they have Caroline's Salon, but according to the owner, there are only two men in town who frequent her establishment."

It wasn't always this way. For four decades, Bill Curtis cut hair in his shop on the town square. After his passing in 1996, most folks either went to Springfield or had a family member cut their hair at home.

Frank, a sophisticated, good-looking 38-year-old, came into town unannounced and set up shop in the space previously occupied by Bill's Barber Shop. With one barber's chair, eight chairs for customers, a table for checkers and a window overlooking Main Street, Frank had all he needed.

It didn't take long for my friend, Marty, and me to find "Frank's Haircuts." My dad told me to get a haircut, and Marty tagged along. We were enamored with Frank right away.

He was funny, but in a sophisticated kind of way. He was very polite and even called us by our last names.

When talking to Marty, he'd say something like, "Mr. McPherson, did anything interesting happen at school today?"

He had a big-screen TV, bigger than any of us had ever seen before. The screen was 34 inches, and it sat on a wooden stand to the left of the customer chairs.

There were two rules when we visited Frank's. First, we were always to be polite to customers who came in while we were there. Second, we weren't to touch the TV.

Most days, we hung out at the barbershop from 3:45 until 4:30, when Frank closed. That meant we saw the last half of *Mayberry RFD* and an episode of *The Andy Griffith Show*, Frank's favorite program.

None of us had ever watched *Andy Griffith* before Frank came along. It was something our parents grew up watching, but we were members of the MTV generation.

Once, during Frank's second week in business, just as Gomer was screaming, "Citizen's arrest!" on the TV, we turned to see Sarah Hyden-Smith, pastor of Lennox Valley Methodist Church, enter the barber shop.

Frank, who was cutting Earl Goodman's hair, stood silent for a moment before welcoming her to the shop. "Hi, I'm Frank Bell. What can I do for you?"

Marty spoke up, "Do you need a haircut, Rev. Smith?"

Everybody laughed.

Sarah laughed with us, then explained she dropped by to meet our newest citizen.

"We'd love to have you visit our church sometime," she said.

She sounded different than usual. Her voice seemed more girlish, less ministerial. She fiddled with her hair as she waited for his response.

Thankfully, Barney shouted something funny to Gomer on the TV.

Finally, Frank answered, "I think I'd like that."

As Sarah made her way down the sidewalk, Frank stood, with a stunned look on his face.

"Are you OK?" Marty finally asked.

Frank smiled and responded, "Boys, I've never been better."

Chapter Eighteen

OCTOBER 1998

Ulterior Motive

New Barber Has More Than Church on His Mind

After nine days in business in his new hometown, Frank Bell had begun to wonder if he had made the right decision. Business was okay, and local high school students enjoyed having a place to hang out after school. A few had even gotten haircuts.

Living in a place like The Valley had its drawbacks. Teenagers weren't the only residents who couldn't find much to do in our town.

Most activities revolved around churches, and most of those revolved around married couples and families. Other than church functions, entertainment was primarily limited to the few civic clubs in town.

On Wednesday, Frank had something else on his mind – the young Methodist minister who dropped by his barber shop the day before to invite him to her church.

Frank wasn't a regular churchgoer in the big city where he lived before The Valley. In Terra Haute, he worked most days and spent evenings with friends, going to ball games, movies or whatever. That's not to say he never attended church, and in a place like Lennox Valley, chances are he would have made his way into one of the four congregations before too long.

For some reason, Frank couldn't get Rev. Sarah Hyden-Smith off his mind. At 10 a.m., he made the decision to call Sarah and take her up on the offer to visit her church.

He hoped Sarah would remember him from their earlier conversation. "Rev. Smith," remembering what one of the boys called her in the shop on Tuesday, "This is Frank Bell. We met at my barber shop yesterday."

The reminder wasn't necessary. Ministers in small towns aren't as busy as folks often imagine. In Frank's mind, Sarah was hurriedly rushing from one crisis to the next. Perhaps a lost soul was being saved, a dying parishioner was being comforted, or a soul-stirring sermon was being prepared on this ordinary Wednesday morning.

"I was thinking about what you said yesterday, and I think you're right. It would be a good idea for me to visit your church."

"Well, that's wonderful," answered Sarah, not correcting him concerning her name. "Our service is at 11. If you're interested, we have Sunday School at 10."

Frank had other thoughts. "I was thinking it might be a good idea for me come by the church before Sunday." After a pause, he continued, "so I'll know where to go when I get there."

Sarah cheerfully agreed to meet Frank at the church just after noon. It was a short walk from his shop, which was closed for the traditional lunch hour each day.

Upon his arrival, a quick tour of the church ensued. Frank could now find his way to the sanctuary, the Sunday school room and the fellowship hall, where coffee was served before the worship service.

They each took a seat in the sanctuary, Sarah seated in the pew in front of Frank.

"Do you have a favorite hymn?" she asked, trying to make conversation. Sarah was probably as excited about meeting Frank as he was about meeting her.

She quickly realized his struggle as he tried to come up with a suitable answer.

"I'll bet you're a fan of Charles Wesley," she said. "He wrote so many good ones."

"He sure did," answered Frank, not having any idea who Charles Wesley was. Frank didn't want to lie to his newfound friend, but decided it must be true if she thought so highly of Wesley.

Eventually Frank found the nerve to ask Sarah if she'd like to have lunch with him at the Hoffbrau. It was just 12:20, and he didn't have to be back at the shop at the stroke of 1 p.m. There were advantages to owning a barber shop across the street from the Hoffbrau and one block down from the Methodist Church.

Over lunch, Sarah shared a little about the town and a little about herself. Like Frank, she was from the big city, albeit a little bigger than Terre Haute.

Her hyphenated name was a result of her marriage 12 years earlier. She simply mentioned her husband had "passed away" and left it at that.

Her stories about Raymond Cooper and his run for the mayor's office left Frank in stitches. He thought she was joking, but eventually realized the stories were true.

Like Frank, Sarah was still new to The Valley, having moved just four months earlier. She mentioned it seemed longer, much longer to her. After a handshake, they parted ways, both silently hoping this would not be the last meal they would share together.

Chapter Nineteen

The Barber Knows

New Shop Rivals 'Brau for Inside Scoop

Being a barber is a lot like being a priest, or even a bartender. Customers might tell you anything: a funny story, a lesson in town history, or even their deepest, darkest secrets. It is an almost sacred calling.

There's something about sitting in a barber's chair that seems oddly familiar. For many, climbing on the booster stool is one of our earliest childhood memories. The sound of clippers and the feel of the brush on the back of your neck conjures recollections of a bygone era.

When the barber clips the black vinyl drape around your neck, it's almost impossible for your mind to keep from wandering back to years long gone.

Frank Bell opened his shop on Main Street less than two weeks earlier, yet in that time he had learned enough about the good folks of Lennox Valley to fill a couple of novels had he been a writer. After living most of his life in the "big city" of Terre Haute, Indiana, Frank was starting to feel like he knew more intimate details of The Valley after two weeks than he learned about his former home in 38 years.

Between his new clientele, tales from the teenagers who hung out in the shop after school and his visit two days earlier with Sarah, pastor of the Methodist Church, Frank was becoming somewhat of an authority on town history. It wouldn't be long before he would be as confused as everyone else concerning the seemingly constant drama surrounding his new home.

Speaking of constant drama, Iris Long was at wits' end trying to decide how to handle the recent departure of her former friend and columnist, Maxine Miller. Maxine's column was perhaps the most popular regular feature in *The Hometown News*. Losing "Rumor Has It" to her nemesis-turned-rival newspaper publisher, Raymond Cooper, had left more than a hole in her newspaper.

Iris had been in the news business a long time, and she quickly moved past the personal betrayal. Seated in her regular booth, staring at the Hoffbrau menu, she was most worried she would soon lose even more readers to Cooper's "rag" if she didn't come up with a suitable replacement for "Rumor Has It."

Dr. Palpant recommended Iris watch her food intake, as the stress of the recent election and new business competition had led to a good bit of "emotional eating," as he called it. Iris had done a good job for more than a week, but continued thoughts of her newspaper going under led her to turn to the Signature French Toast for comfort.

If two slices of egg-battered sourdough bread, toasted on the griddle until golden brown and sprinkled with powdered sugar, couldn't calm Long's nerves, perhaps nothing would.

It was hard to think at the moment, however, as she waited on her food. Jessie, her waitress and friend, was talking nonstop concerning the latest gossip she overheard during the breakfast rush an hour earlier.

Elbert Lee Jones had seen the new barber walking with Sarah Hyden-Smith to lunch at the 'Brau on Wednesday. Vera Pinrod was sure she had seen Raymond Cooper with A.J. Fryerson in Springfield during the Auburn Hat Society meeting at the Red Lobster.

The hem of Rhonda Graham's dress at Sunday services was no less than two inches above her knees, and "Everyone knows Brother Billy Joe doesn't approve of such shameless attire at his church."

Jessie's rambling almost caused Iris to lose her temper. That's when it hit her.

"Jessie," Iris interrupted, "have you ever thought of becoming a writer?"

"What in the world are you talking about?" Jessie replied.

"Yes, I think you just might have a new career," Iris said with a slight grin.

Chapter Twenty

Maxine's Problem

Some Things are Changing in The Valley

Maxine Miller was more than a little concerned. For the past 20 years she had gotten her best material for "Rumor Has It" from Jessie Taylor, waitress at the Hoffbrau. Jessie overheard the conversations of just about everyone in town as she refilled coffees and served blue plate specials. Between Jessie's insights and A.J. Fryerson's complaints, Maxine always seemed to have enough material for her weekly column.

Those who didn't know Jessie very well might have been surprised by her thoughtful insights. More than once, Maxine picked up on something Jessie said and wrote it as her own.

In 1992, she penned words still taped to refrigerator doors throughout The Valley. "Sometimes you find yourself in the middle of nowhere, and sometimes in the middle of nowhere, you find yourself."

By late October, something had changed. Maxine assumed Jessie was upset by Miller's betrayal of Iris Long, editor of *The Hometown News*. Now, when Maxine pried for information, Jessie either pretended not to notice or answered, "I wouldn't know."

Richard Armour, humorist, is remembered for his 1949 quote, "Hindsight is 20-20." Maxine was starting to think Armour was on to something. She was beginning to wonder if jumping ship to write for Raymond Cooper's paper had been a good idea after all.

Sources for material were drying up. It seemed Iris had a lot of friends in The Valley. To make matters worse, after only two issues, *The Valley Patriot* seemed to be losing steam. The Tuesday publication needed help immediately.

While not poor by any means, Raymond Cooper couldn't keep producing a paper with almost no paid advertising. If he wanted the folks of Lennox Valley to read his paper, he would eventually have to write about something besides Iris Long, A.J. Fryerson and himself.

With no photographer, no writers, no designers and no editors, other than himself, *The Patriot* already looked like what it was – a worthless rag created to stroke the ego of Raymond Cooper and punish his long-time rival, Iris Long. The table of contents for his third issue amplified Maxine's concerns:

Local News . . . . *Page 1*

Raymond's Renderings . . . . . *Pages 2-3*

Rumor Has It . . . . *Page 6*

Opinion Page . . . . *Page 6*

Church News . . . . *Page 7*

Political Review. . . . . *Page 7*

Classifieds. . . . . *Page 7*

The table of contents now took up the full bottom-right quarter of the page. Local news consisted of an A.J. Fryerson update, a brief story about the new barber in town and an interview with Earl Goodman concerning the upcoming postal increase, from 32 cents to 33 cents, for a first-class stamp. The only photo on the front page was of Goodman holding a blank postcard with the caption, "Postcard rates are still a bargain!"

Pages 4 and 5 were filled with an ad for Farley Puckett's Hardware Store. It was the only paid ad in the issue, costing Farley all of $35. Page 8 was a full page ad for Cooper's radio show.

Maxine's column was already showing signs of decline. Her juiciest tidbit involved Frank Bell. "It seems our new barber found a place on the second row at the Methodist Church this week," she began. "Could it be his eyesight is failing from staring so closely at hair all week, or could something else, or someone, be the motivation for his proximity to the pulpit?"

Yes, Maxine was worried as she sat in her booth at the 'Brau on Wednesday morning, waiting for the latest issue of *The Hometown News* to arrive. She wondered if it was too late to ask Iris for her old job back, assuming Long would ever forgive her.

Not wanting to seem too anxious, Maxine waited a few minutes after a stack of newspapers landed on the counter. Opening her copy, her face turned flush as she saw the headline on page 2:

Did You Hear?
Scoops from a reliable source

"Are you all right?" Diane Curtis asked from across the aisle. "You look like you saw a ghost."

"I may have," whispered Miller. "My own."

Chapter Twenty-One

OCTOBER 1998

Valley Constable

Frank Bell Gets the Inside Scoop

After three weeks in The Valley, Frank Bell thought he had heard just about everything. My hometown was a lot to take in, even for someone like me who was born and raised there. Just imagine moving from a big city like Terre Haute, Indiana, to our small town.

In the beginning, Frank got most of his information from my group of friends, as we found our way to his barber shop just about every day after school. His only real adult friend so far was Rev. Sarah Hyden-Smith, who dropped by to invite Frank to visit the Methodist church. That invitation led to a "scandalous rendezvous," according to Maxine Miller's "Rumor Has It" column, over lunch at the Hoffbrau.

Things were starting to pick up after three weeks in business. Several of The Valley's good folks had dropped by for cuts and, as is often the case, to discuss the news of the day.

Though Raymond Cooper hadn't been to the shop yet, Frank was already familiar with his antics. Stories of Raymond's near victory in the recent mayoral election, his miraculous conversion during the 8:30 morning service at the Lutheran church and the pig stampede at the county fair made Cooper seem larger than life to our town's newest citizen.

On Thursday, Constable Erby Bailey laughed out loud as he told a series of Raymond Cooper stories.

"You know," Bailey whispered, as if sharing a secret, "this is confidential information."

"Of course," Frank answered, trying to look as solemn as possible while attempting to hold in his laughter.

Constables, I later learned, are elected officials who operate as officers at no cost to the county. They do, however, get a kickback from the state for writing citations, making arrests and serving court summons. The state-based fee for each service at that time was $1 per citation, $10 per arrest and $5 for each summons.

"I've never cited anyone for not wearing their seat belt," he said, obviously interested in more serious offenses. "And you can ask anybody, I rarely give a speeding ticket unless the driver is going 10 miles over the limit."

"But it was like this," the good constable continued, "I was on Highway 11 a couple of weeks ago and noticed this car driving a good 15 miles over the limit. I didn't notice at first, because it was dark, it was Raymond Cooper in the driver's seat."

"Did you give him a ticket?" Frank asked, trying to act as if he was really interested in the story.

"I'm getting to that part," Bailey answered, obviously enamored with his own story. He continued, "I said, 'Raymond, where are you going in such a hurry?'"

That's when the constable explained how he noticed Raymond seemed a bit fidgety and upset at the same time. Erby saw someone in the passenger's seat. He couldn't make out who it was in the dark, and he wasn't about to use his flashlight. Raymond was already irritated enough.

"Raymond told me he had been in Springfield to cover a big story for his newspaper," Bailey continued. "He said he needed to get back to the paper to write the story in time for the next issue, so I apologized for the delay and told him to be careful, since he was so tired."

"That was nice of you," Frank responded to the confidential information.

Then Erby held his left hand in the air, as if telling Frank to stop what he was doing for a moment. "The funny thing is," Bailey spoke carefully, "there weren't any stories about Springfield in his next paper."

"That is peculiar," Frank answered.

Just then the bell above the door jingled, putting a stop to any talk of Raymond Cooper.

"Well, hello, Pastor!" Erby shouted as Brother Billy Joe Prather entered the shop.

After a quick introduction, Billy Joe got right to the point.

"I wanted to welcome you to The Valley," he said gleefully to Frank. "I assume you'll make a visit to First Baptist Church. It's The Valley's largest congregation, you know."

The pastor continued, "And I'm sure you'll want to attend our annual men's breakfast and turkey shoot next month."

"A turkey shoot?" asked Frank.

"Yes, the biggest in the county," Billy Joe answered proudly.

"I guess I haven't heard everything after all," Frank thought to himself.

Chapter Twenty-Two

OCTOBER 1998

We've Got Trouble!

Right Here in Lennox Valley

A stranger passing through Lennox Valley would naturally think there wasn't much going on during my growing years. In fact, I would be hard pressed to name a single uneventful week in my hometown. Whenever it seemed as if the drama was settling, something would happen to stir our emotions in a big way.

Raymond Cooper was responsible for more than his fair share of stirring. I can't imagine what The Valley might have been like during those years without him.

Most would have thought Raymond would settle down after his narrow defeat in the mayor's race. However, there he was, two months later, mixing up as much trouble as ever.

As usual, Cooper devised a villainous scheme to guarantee a steady audience for his radio show, "Renderings With Raymond," while also boosting readership of his weekly rag, *The Valley Patriot*.

Declining interest in *The Patriot* was the cause of much concern to Raymond in late October, though he never admitted it. To hear him talk, his "newspaper" was about to topple Iris Long's *Hometown News* and would soon be in line for a Pulitzer or two.

Concerned about his "baby," he came up with a sinister plan. Cooper and Maxine Miller, of "Rumor Has It" fame, wrote most of the copy in *The Valley Patriot*, and Maxine reported directly to Raymond.

Cooper quickly realized by including stories in *The Patriot,* then using his radio show to galvanize the audience, he could exploit the most insignificant "scoop," turning it into a matter of national urgency.

As readers scrutinized the front page of *The Valley Patriot* on October 27, 1998, they soon learned their peaceful village was under attack from exterior forces. There were two main stories, plus a brief update of the A.J. Fryerson drama and the Table of Contents.

Filling the bottom-left area of the page was a headline in 28-point type:

Baptists Take Turkeys to Task in Upcoming Event

The story was nearly a carbon copy of one found a year earlier in *The Hometown News* regarding the annual Men's Breakfast and Turkey Shoot at First Baptist Church.

A more ominous headline filled two lines stretched across the top of the page. In 80-point type, the apocalyptic banner read, "Foreign Power Attempts to Manipulate Valley Youth!"

Imagine the newspaper headlines proclaiming the end of World War II, and you have a fairly good idea of the impact of Cooper's story.

Valley residents couldn't help but pick up Raymond's paper after seeing the headline. The story detailed an evil book that had made its way across the Atlantic directly into the hands of Valley teenagers.

Harry Potter and the Sorcerer's Stone was the rage among teenagers in Britain and, as Raymond "uncovered," was gaining steam among high school and, in some cases, middle school students living in The Valley.

Cooper ignored the fact he had dismissed the book six months earlier saying, "It's nothing to worry about. It will be forgotten in a couple of weeks."

At the time, Raymond was more concerned about getting himself elected. However, the book now was growing more popular by the day and was perfect fodder to stir the emotions of the listening, and reading, public.

Cooper's guest on Tuesday's show was Brother Jacob, associate pastor at the Lutheran church. It took only a moment for Jacob to regret accepting the invitation.

"How do you feel about evil forces attacking our children, Pastor?" Raymond almost shouted.

Brother Jacob thought for a moment. He had been the victim of Cooper's on-air manipulation before.

"Well, no one wants evil forces attacking anyone, especially our children," Jacob responded. "But . . ."

Cooper jumped in before the pastor could finish his sentence.

"You heard Brother Jacob. Sinister forces are attacking our children. I ask you, where is our so-called mayor while all this is taking place?"

Jacob tried to jump in, but Raymond would have nothing of it. After a moment Raymond thanked him for being on the show and urged his listeners to visit Jacob's 8:30 service some Sunday morning.

"It is, after all," Raymond whispered, "where I was converted."

It wasn't the first time Brother Jacob wished Cooper had been converted at the Methodist or Baptist church.

Chapter Twenty-Three

OCTOBER 1998

Sign of the Times

Baptist Billboard Generates Cutting Remarks

While looking over the location before signing the lease for his new barber shop, Frank Bell immediately noticed the panoramic view just outside the sizable front window of the establishment. From the barber's chair, a customer could see a good portion of the town square.

Looking across the square diagonally, Frank and his clientele had a clear view of Bearden's Corner, famous for the four churches which called the site home. Just up the street, almost directly across the square from Frank's shop, was the Hoffbrau.

Following his visit to the Methodist church the previous Sunday, Frank thought it was funny seeing the Lutherans leaving church and walking directly over to the 'Brau for lunch. As he walked around the square a few times, hoping Sarah Hyden-Smith might make an appearance, he noticed the members of First Baptist Church leaving about 20 minutes later.

"Funny," he thought. "None of the Baptists seem to be walking over to the Hoffbrau."

Little did he know that Brother Billy Joe had a firm rule against his congregants having lunch or dinner at the 'Brau through the week. Most Baptists had decided breakfast was okay, since beer wasn't generally served during the early morning hours.

It was Friday, and you can be sure Caroline's Salon was "filled to the brim" with ladies having their hair done for upcoming Sunday services. Some mothers would bring their sons to Frank's for a Friday afternoon cut, but most working men reserved Saturdays for their grooming, which tended to happen sporadically at best.

Elbert Lee Jones was having his hair cut when he gazed across the square at Iris Long, who seemed to be taking a picture.

"You see that?" Elbert Lee asked Frank. "That's Iris Long. She runs the newspaper in town."

After a pause, he continued. "Well, I guess I should say she runs one of the newspapers in town."

Jones wasn't about to forget his old friend, Raymond Cooper, the town's newest publisher.

"He must have done it again," Elbert Lee offered with a chuckle.

"Done what?" Frank asked innocently.

"That Loren McBeevy," Jones answered. "He changes the sign in front of First Baptist Church two or three times a week."

Elbert Lee chuckled again before continuing. "He has a habit of not paying enough attention to what he's putting on the sign. A couple of years ago, he was putting up the sign and forgot about the pastor's name being on the bottom. He's done that more than once."

Jones stopped to laugh before continuing. "When he finished putting up the letters, it read, 'Who's the biggest sinner?' Then underneath was 'Brother Billy Joe Prather.'"

"I'll tell you," Elbert Lee continued, "We laughed about that for a month, and it was about that long before Billy Joe let Loren put up another sign."

Frank made a mental note to check out the sign when he had a free minute.

As he was sweeping the floor following Elbert Lee's cut, Frank heard the familiar bell ring above the door, meaning someone was walking in.

"I just thought I'd check on our newest citizen," Sarah Hyden-Smith said with a grin. She wasn't doing a very good job containing her pleasure. "You haven't turned Lutheran on us this week, have you?"

86

Frank laughed before answering, "No, but I'm thinking I might become Baptist if the sign appeals to me today."

He explained to Sarah about watching Iris Long take a picture of the sign, so they decided to take a walk across the square to see what all the fuss was about.

As they crossed the square, it was obvious they weren't the first to take interest in Loren's latest work. There were close to a dozen folks laughing and pointing at the sign as they approached.

Apparently, Brother Billy Joe had instructed Loren to promote the upcoming men's breakfast and turkey shoot.

There it was for everyone to see, and Frank was so glad he had a chance to see it before Brother Billy Joe had it removed.

"Best breakfast in town! Come and eat."

Just below those words were, "Brother Billy Joe Prather."

Sarah laughed out loud. It was the perfect second date.

Chapter Twenty-Four

OCTOBER 1998

Silver Tongue

Dick Bland Lived the Name

Mayor Dick "Silver Tongue" Bland enjoyed a brief period of respite for a few short weeks following his narrow victory in the August election. It wasn't long, however, before his old nemesis was making life miserable once again.

Everyone has a breaking point, and Mayor Bland had reached his. For weeks, since Raymond Cooper returned to the air and launched his weekly "newspaper," Silver Tongue remained silent as he heard his former rival blame him for everything from A.J. Fryerson's disappearance to the rapid demise of morals among Valley teens as a result of the rising popularity of *Harry Potter and the Sorcerer's Stone.*

Bland was "fit to be tied" as he entered Frank's Barber Shop to get a trim before his hastily arranged town hall meeting. Frank had just returned from lunch as the mayor walked into the shop.

"What in the world is going on over at the Baptist church?" Bland asked Frank.

"Oh, Loren mistakenly announced the pastor would be the main course for breakfast in two weeks," Frank answered, referring to the poorly arranged words on the Baptist church sign.

As they peered out the window across the square, they could see the Baptist youth minister removing the letters from the sign as onlookers watched.

Silver Tongue had seen Loren's handiwork before and didn't seem surprised. Anyway, he had something more important on his mind.

The mayor was no political rookie. He knew Cooper was back to his old ways, and Bland was adept at playing the political game.

Raymond's show would be off the air in ten minutes. In 40 minutes, the mayor would be standing in the assembly room of the Town Hall, making a statement to the good folks of The Valley. He wanted to look just right, which included getting his hair trimmed for the event.

As Frank carefully snipped, Bland shared his insights, letting Frank know he would be wise to steer clear of Raymond Cooper.

"He's a sore spot in our community," Silver Tongue told Frank. "He's like a piece of gum that just won't come off your shoe sole."

They didn't call him "Silver Tongue" for nothing.

"Yes, he's been stuck to my shoe for too long, and he can't stand that I defeated him convincingly in the last election."

Frank rarely listened to the radio and had yet to pick up Cooper's rag, *The Valley Patriot*. What he knew of Raymond he'd learned from his new best friend, Sarah-Hyden Smith, and from customers who would mention Cooper's name now and then.

"I'll remember that," he told the mayor, attempting to keep his customer happy.

The mayor told Frank he should close the shop for a few minutes at 3:30 to attend the gathering at the Town Hall. "Everybody will be there, so you won't lose any business."

At precisely 3:30, the mayor stood behind the hall's stage lectern.

"Friends," he began, "I feel the need to set some things straight." Using a line borrowed from Abe Lincoln, he continued. "A house divided against itself cannot stand."

"Over the past weeks, I have decided to 'speak softly, and carry a big stick,'" borrowing a line from Teddy Roosevelt. "I want you to know," he continued, "the buck stops here," sounding a lot like Harry Truman.

The assembly of 200 or so townsfolk roared their approval. Silver

Tongue sure knew how to work up a crowd.

He continued. "As for the reading material of our youth, let our families and beloved clergy be the judges of what is proper and what is not, and let me assure you that our community is safe. We have no evidence there is any foul play in the disappearance of one of our citizens. For all we know, he may be visiting a distant relative as I speak."

As the applause grew in volume, he waited patiently for the crowd to quiet down.

"I shall defend our Valley, whatever the cost may be. I will fight for every Valley citizen, in the fields and in the streets. I will fight in the hills. I will never surrender."

The crowd could barely contain itself.

Mayor Bland felt the tide of emotions turn in his favor. But as Silver Tongue smiled a wide smile at the Town Hall, Raymond was scheming with an audience of one, 15 miles away on the other side of Springfield.

Chapter Twenty-Five

OCTOBER 1998

Tempers Flare

Following Silver Tongue's Dirty Trick

Marvin Walsh was fit to be tied on Saturday morning. So was Earl Goodman, the town's only federal employee.

"What a low-down, dirty trick," Marvin yelled as he waved his hands toward the ceiling in disgust. "I never thought Silver Tongue would sink so low."

As the two men sat in the lobby of 880 AM, Lennox Valley's only radio station, they discussed the events of Friday afternoon which led to their mutual discontent.

"What a low-down, dirty trick," echoed Earl, barely able to contain himself. "Bland knew by giving that speech on Friday afternoon, Raymond wouldn't have a chance to defend himself before Monday."

"You should do something about it," shouted Marvin.

"Me? Why should I do something about it?" asked Goodman, still raising his voice.

Walsh offered the obvious answer, "Because you're a federal employee. Silver Tongue is a city employee. Surely a fed trumps a local when it comes to these matters."

Marvin couldn't quite comprehend the fact that postal carriers didn't carry a lot of weight in government issues. Tempers were about to flare as Raymond Cooper entered the room.

"Boys, what's all the fuss about?" quizzed Raymond.

"What's all the fuss about?" Marvin screamed before asking again, "What's all the fuss about? You want to know what all the fuss is about? Didn't you hear what Silver Tongue said yesterday?"

Neither Walsh nor Goodman knew Raymond was involved in an important secret meeting 15 miles away in Springfield during Bland's speech.

"I was on out-of-town business. What did he have to say?" Cooper asked, as if he didn't already know.

"First," Earl exploded, "he said the reading habits of children weren't any of the government's business. He said only parents and preachers should have a say in what our youth can and can't read."

"Then," Marvin jumped in, before Earl could continue, "he said A.J. Fryerson was probably on some kind of vacation, visiting family." After a sigh, he continued, "Everybody knows A.J. didn't have any family."

"That is mighty peculiar," Raymond said, rubbing his chin. "I wonder what makes him think that."

Walsh was quick with an answer. "You know Silver Tongue. He doesn't know a thing. He's just tired of you making him look so bad. You are the only one in this town looking for answers."

"Each of us," Cooper interjected, "has a responsibility to our community. With great power comes great responsibility."

At that moment, both Marvin and Earl were reminded they were in the presence of greatness.

"And," Marvin continued, "you know he gave that speech on Friday afternoon, after your show, knowing you wouldn't get a chance to defend yourself until Monday."

"What a low-down, dirty trick," Earl chimed in.

"It is," shouted Walsh. "It's a low-down, dirty trick."

Raymond took control. "Well, boys, it is a shame our so-called mayor feels like he has to stoop so low. It's important, however, that we not stoop down to his level."

As Iris Long, editor of *The Hometown News*, walked past the front of the radio station, she glanced in to see the three men in deep conversation.

"Oh, my," she thought to herself, "I wonder what those three are cooking up."

Ten minutes later, Raymond adjourned the impromptu meeting by saying, "I think we all know what we have to do."

Looking toward Earl, he said, "Earl, don't forget your lines." Then, looking over at Marvin, he barked, "You know what you're supposed to do."

As they walked out the front door of the radio station, Iris, who was standing in the doorway of the Hoffbrau, heard Marvin say, "I'll see you at church," which was peculiar, knowing Raymond hadn't attended church since the mayoral election.

"Hmm," she whispered to herself. "What are they up to now?"

Chapter Twenty-Six

Marvin and Raymond

More Than the Spirit is Moving at Church

More often than not, Sunday was the most anticipated day of the week in The Valley. It's not because anything earth-shattering took place in the four sanctuaries each week, but most folks like having people and places in their lives which don't change significantly over time, and the Sunday morning service was just such a place.

Sure, people come and go. In time, even priests and preachers either move on or pass away. Still, it was soothing to know most things remained the same from week to week and year to year.

At the Lennox Valley Methodist Church, Sarah Hyden-Smith was making last-minute preparations for the morning worship service. She came in early on Sundays, usually around 6:30 a.m., to make sure everything was ready for Sunday school and worship. She glanced over the bulletin Becky Moorehouse, part-time church secretary and bookkeeper, had prepared.

The Methodists count on certain activities. Normally, they began with announcements and then sing an opening hymn, usually written by Charles Wesley, brother of Methodism's founder, John Wesley. Like the Catholic church across the corner, the fine Methodists of Lennox Valley would dutifully recite the Apostle's Creed midway through the service.

As Sarah made her final preparations for the morning, Father O'Reilly had already begun the first of two services. The Catholics referred to their worship service as a Mass, which made most of the Baptists and even some Methodists wonder what was actually going on within the walls of All Saints Church. The first Mass, at 8 a.m., was held in Latin, while English was spoken at the 10:30 Mass.

At 8:25, Brother Billy Joe Prather made his way to his chair, located directly behind the pulpit of First Baptist Church. Brother Billy Joe didn't use notes as he preached, so he used these last few minutes to pray for inspiration as he led his flock.

The Baptists, like the Catholics and Lutherans, held two services on Sunday morning. Being exactly six days before October 31, Brother Billy Joe would firmly remind his congregation to do their trick-or-treating early on Saturday night while being careful to wear suitable costumes. He suggested Moses, Mary and David were especially appropriate characters, allowing children to share in the holiday festivities while evangelizing to their community at the same time.

One day earlier, Iris Long overheard Marvin Walsh telling his friends Raymond Cooper and Earl Goodman, "See you in church."

Regardless of countless references to his scriptural prowess and spiritual leadership on his radio show, Iris knew Raymond never attended worship, other than a few visits to the Lutheran church just before the mayoral election. She also knew Marvin hadn't been a regular churchgoer in years, having become upset when First Baptist began singing "rock and roll" songs in church back in the 70s. He especially disliked "Kumbaya," having no idea what the song was about, prompting several letters to the editor of *The Hometown News*.

Iris guessed if Raymond was to meet Marvin in church, it would be at the contemporary service at Valley Lutheran Church. It was, after all, the place Cooper experienced his "great conversion" just prior to the election.

At 8:28, Brother Jacob welcomed Iris as she entered the fellowship hall where the contemporary service was held. Visitors were rare at the 8:30 service and were greeted warmly. She had been to the service once before, taking a photo and writing a story about the new service for *The Hometown News*. She now took a seat in the back row of folding metal chairs.

Iris counted 14 folks in attendance as the electronic keyboard began to play, but there was no Raymond Cooper nor Marvin Walsh in sight. At 8:32, she heard some type of commotion coming from the door behind her. She turned to see Raymond walking in alone, then taking a seat in the third row, one ahead of her, on the far end of the row.

As the congregation stood to sing, "Mighty is Our God," she heard another noise coming from behind. It was Marvin, who had walked into the fellowship hall but seemed to be talking to someone outside the partially open door.

"Good Lord," she murmured. "What are they up to now?"

Chapter Twenty-Seven

NOVEMBER 1998

Somethin's Cookin'

It's a Busy Morning at Valley Churches

Iris Long may have been the only person in The Valley who wasn't surprised by the strange series of events taking place among the various congregations on Bearden's Corner that fateful Sunday in late October. She had a hint something was up on Saturday as she caught a glimpse of Raymond Cooper and his minions making plans in the lobby of Talk Radio 880.

What their plans were, she couldn't be sure. But as she overheard Marvin tell Raymond he would see him in church, she had a feeling they were up to no good.

The next morning, as she sat on the back row during the 8:30 a.m. contemporary service at Lennox Valley Lutheran Church, she was unaware Lutherans weren't the only Christians who were in for a surprise that fateful morning. As Iris turned to see what kind of commotion was taking place at the back door, she heard the keyboard playing, "Mighty is Our God," as the 14 congregants stood and raised their arms in the air.

That's just the kind of thing which would take place in the 8:30 service, but would never transpire two hours later in the traditional worship upstairs. Iris couldn't make out what was being said from behind her as the song leader, Miranda Tessendorf, led the group, repeating the chorus several times.

"Good Lord," Iris murmured to herself. "Do they think God didn't hear them the first 10 times they sang it?"

Over at Lennox Valley Methodist Church, everything seemed to be going swimmingly as folks gathered to prepare coffee and make necessary arrangements for Sunday school, which took place each week before the worship service.

The Catholics and Lutherans never quite understood the affinity Methodists and Baptists had for Sunday school. To the fine folks at All Saints Catholic Church, it was confusing to try to understand why someone would want to attend church twice on the same morning.

The Lutherans had classes for children, along with a Bible study group attended by six or eight adults each week while their offspring were in class, but the whole idea of splitting up into different groups to listen to amateurs teach the Bible just didn't make sense. It was rumored the Baptist church had classes for younger adults, older adults, college students, and even singles.

As James Bretcher once told his fellow Lutherans, "It's beyond me why single folks need a different lesson than married folks. Why not just call it what it is, the church dating service? Lord only knows what they talk about in that class."

As the pianist at the Methodist church practiced playing the morning anthem, "A Charge to Keep I Have," the officers of the Methodist Women's group were busy setting up a table in the narthex for the annual LVMW (Lennox Valley Methodist Women) Cookbook sale.

Trying to keep up with the names for rooms in different churches could get pretty confusing. While the Methodists called the area leading into the sanctuary the "narthex," over at First Baptist it was called the "vestibule," a word that always gave me the shivers.

The Methodist Women officers were especially excited about this particular cookbook because they had a "celebrity" chef submit six recipes for the book. Valerie Pinkin, wife of Channel 6 meteorologist Matt Pinkin, graced the cover, holding her renowned Battenberg cake.

Carol Weems, president of the Methodist Women, had written Mrs. Pinkin to invite her to attend church on "Cookbook Kickoff

Sunday," but Carol hadn't received a response. Still, the officers of the group expected a healthy bump in attendance, as folks would surely show up, just in case. We didn't get many celebrities in The Valley.

Over at First Baptist Church, more than 100 folks joined in singing "When the Roll is Called Up Yonder," as the service began in earnest. One visitor, however, stood quietly, unfamiliar with the song.

Back at the Lutheran church, as Iris Long strained to hear what Marvin Walsh was saying to an unknown listener just outside the door at Lennox Valley Lutheran Church and Carol Weems gleamed in anticipation of another successful Cookbook Sunday, Juliette Stoughton gathered courage for what was about to take place at First Baptist Church.

Chapter Twenty-Eight

Mystery Letter

Could A.J. Have Been Right for a Change?

As Iris Long sat in her seat in the back row of the Lutheran contemporary service, her mind was moving in several different directions at once. Raymond Cooper, seated ten seats to her left on the opposite end of the row, was obviously uncomfortable. She could sense something wasn't going according to plan.

Standing behind her, just inside the entrance to the fellowship hall, Marvin Walsh was noticeably upset as he talked with someone on the other side of the door. It was as if Marvin was trying to coerce someone into the building, but Iris couldn't quite make out his words as the seventh chorus of "Mighty is Our God" burst from the electronic piano located on the platform directly in front of the congregation.

Her mind raced between watching Raymond from the corner of her eye, attempting to make out what was being said behind her, and thinking back to a letter she received from A.J. Fryerson just before his disappearance.

A.J. had been missing for two months. Iris couldn't help but think whatever was going on with Raymond and Marvin was somehow related to A.J. Fryerson. After all, Raymond had spent several hours railing against Mayor Dick Bland and Chief of Police Dibble during the previous week. Raymond blamed the two public servants for not providing answers to citizens who feared for their own safety following the disappearance.

On Friday's "Renderings with Raymond," Cooper was especially aggressive.

"Maybe," Raymond shouted into the microphone, "A.J. was kidnapped!" After a brief pause to let listeners dwell on the thought, he continued, "Maybe he's being tortured as I speak at this very moment."

The speech by Mayor Bland on Friday, assailing those who were creating panic about A.J.'s disappearance with no evidence to suggest foul play, was an obvious attack aimed at his nemesis and former political opponent, Raymond Cooper. Iris had a hunch the meeting between Cooper, Walsh and Earl Goodman, which she unwittingly glimpsed while passing the radio station Saturday morning, had something to do with the mayor's speech and Fryerson.

Her mind travelled back to Saturday morning, as she stood in the entrance to the Hoffbrau, just out of sight of the conspirators as they parted ways. She could still hear Marvin shout, "See you in church!" knowing all along Cooper and Walsh weren't regular churchgoers.

Iris hadn't told anyone about the letter. A.J. penned letters to the editor every week. Sometimes he would write two or three in a week. Never mailing them, he would drop them off at the newspaper office to save himself the 32 cents postage.

She remembered the last time she saw Fryerson. He came by the office early in the morning, as was his practice. Iris often imagined he sat up most of the night to create his latest chef-d'oeuvre.

A.J. seemed especially irritated on that particular morning. Don't misunderstand, he was always irritated. But Iris hadn't seen Fryerson this agitated since his infamous letter-writing feud with Chief Dibble years earlier.

A.J. always seemed to have a comment to add when dropping off his letters. She remembered his initial missive after Buford Levitt installed new pumps at the town's only gas station. After dropping his envelope on *The Hometown News* front counter, he muttered, "That will teach Buford Levitt to steal money from me. He'll think twice before messing with A.J. Fryerson again."

Iris didn't print all of A.J.'s letters. Most readers probably don't realize newspaper publishers are liable for information appearing in a letter to the editor. Whenever Fryerson wrote something that could get *The Hometown News* in hot water with the courts, Iris would file the letter in her "not used" folder. Thanks to A.J., that folder had grown to several folders.

Iris began to feel the ache in her legs as the congregation sang their third "praise song" of the morning. "Don't Lutherans ever sit?" she mumbled to herself.

Iris thought back to Fryerson's final letter which began, "Dear Editor: If other citizens had suffered the way I've suffered, thanks to our chief of police and mayor, they would have left this town a long time ago. As for me, I will stay as long as I have breath in my body."

Chapter Twenty-Nine

NOVEMBER 1998

Marvin Silenced!

Like Lot's Wife, Walsh Frozen in Time

As the eighth chorus of "Mighty is Our God" came to an end, Iris could hear Marvin Walsh verbally struggling at the door 20 feet behind her. With the electronic piano mercifully silent, it was obvious Marvin was having some kind of argument with whoever was outside the door.

Brother Jacob was doing his best to continue the service as usual, though he could see Marvin pointing his finger at someone or something and could hear his muted voice, even at the front of the fellowship hall.

Among other things, October 25 was Reformation Sunday, the official day when Lutherans are allowed to feel superior to everyone else. Lutherans aren't alone in having their own special day. Catholics have the Feast of the Ascension, marking the ascension of Christ to heaven a few weeks after Easter. Methodists have Aldersgate Day, celebrating the day John Wesley's heart felt strangely warmed at Aldersgate, and Baptists have Billy Graham's birthday on November 7.

Marking Martin Luther's break from the Roman Catholic Church, Lutherans everywhere consider Reformation Day the third most important day of the Christian year, behind Easter and Christmas.

As Brother Jacob began the celebration, the church became silent when Marvin shouted, "No!" from the back of the room.

At that moment, you could have heard a pin drop on the tile floor. Brother Jacob gazed at Walsh, who by now realized what he had done. Everyone in the congregation turned to see who was yelling behind them.

Walsh stood there, not moving, in stunned silence. It was apparent he hadn't meant to make such a disturbance. Whomever or whatever was outside the door had incited Marvin's outburst.

Iris Long looked over at Raymond Cooper, fidgeting in the folding metal chair at the opposite end of her row. It was clear the day wasn't going as planned.

"What ARE they up to?" Iris asked herself again.

She had a hunch something was going to happen, and it looked like she was right. She waited along with the rest of the congregation as Marvin stood in silence. After what seemed like minutes, but was actually only a few seconds, Brother Jacob finally spoke.

"Are you OK, Mr. Walsh?"

Marvin was frozen in place, unwilling or unable to speak. The congregation continued to stare at him as his eyes began to ricochet between them, Brother Jacob, and Raymond Cooper.

Iris was quite familiar with Cooper's schemes by now, and she turned to see how he would respond to Walsh's predicament. As usual, he didn't let her down.

"Brother Jacob!" Raymond shouted, gathering the attention of the congregation. "I believe I know what has happened to Marvin."

Jacob, still shocked by Walsh's outburst, slowly moved his eyes from Marvin to Raymond without saying a word. Like Iris, the young Lutheran pastor had learned much about Raymond Cooper in just two years. At this point, there was almost nothing Raymond might do that would surprise his pastor.

Raymond continued. "Just yesterday, Marvin shared with me his need to return to the church. He explained much of his desire to return was kindled by the positive influence of our new associate pastor."

Cooper waited, expecting a response from Brother Jacob. Realizing no response was forthcoming, he continued.

"Marvin called me just last night and told me what had happened to him since making the decision to return to this spiritual haven. He said he could feel the Good Lord speaking to him, telling him to get back to church. But at the same time, he could feel the Devil pulling at him, doing his best to keep him from joining us in worship on this special day. I suppose the Devil knew the celebration of Reformation Sunday might be just the thing to bring Marvin into the fold."

"So I told him," Raymond continued, "If that Devil tries to hold you back, look him straight in the eye and shout 'No!'"

The congregation listened in stunned silence as Raymond spoke.

"I believe, Brother Jacob, that is exactly what happened just now."

"Good Lord," Iris muttered to herself. "He's done it again."

Chapter Thirty

NOVEMBER 1998

Stirring Up the Church

Woman Shakes Up First Baptist Service

There are countless adjectives to describe my hometown. Near the top of almost anyone's list of Valley descriptions, including my own, would be "religious."

Talk to any old-timer about memorable events at area churches, and a few notable memories rise to the top. In the 1930s, a female Pentecostal minister came through town as part of a "Holy Ghost Revival." The evangelist, it was told, dressed in a police uniform, sat in the saddle of a police motorcycle and blew the siren over and over. According to the story, the motorcycle engine made a deafening roar as she drove across the access ramp to the pulpit, slammed on the brakes, then raised a white gloved hand as she shouted, "Stop! You're speeding to Hell!"

More recently, most remember Todd Cecil's visit to Lennox Valley in 1998. It was rare a celebrity made it to my hometown, but it happened twice in 1998 when both Cecil, a famous TV evangelist from Missouri, and singing sensation Tangi Blevins made appearances in our town.

In June of that same year, Rev. Sarah Hyden-Smith arrived, perhaps topping the all-time list of momentous events in the life of Valley churches. Let's face it, those Methodists – with their reputation for peace and composure – sure know how to stir things up.

Theologians and historians refer to three main periods of "Great Awakening" in American religious history. The first was ushered in by the great British evangelist George Whitefield, when he arrived in the early 1700s to spread the gospel to America.

The second "Great Awakening" occurred in the first half of the 19th century, resulting in several reform movements such as temperance, abolition, and women's rights.

The third "Great Awakening," which took place in the second half of the same century, was marked with the creation of several denominations still prevalent today, although they are not so prevalent in Lennox Valley.

As Clarence Southerland once wrote in a letter to the editor of *The Hometown News* when rumor spread a non-denominational church might be coming to town, "We've got enough religion in The Valley. If you can't find what you're looking for in the Baptist, Methodist, Lutheran, or Catholic church, then let me urge you to go to some other town to find it."

I would suggest America's fourth "Great Awakening" took place in Lennox Valley in 1998. Between Todd Cecil, Sarah Hyden-Smith and the events on Reformation Sunday at First Baptist Church, a lot of what we had become accustomed to would be changed forever.

True enough, Baptists don't usually celebrate Reformation Sunday. That's normally reserved for the Lutherans among us. But as Juliette Stoughton rose from her seat upon hearing Brother Billy Joe Prather offer the invitation to come to the altar as the congregation began singing "Pass Me Not, O Gentle Savior," some things would never be the same again.

It was often said Billy Joe's smile was so bright, the reflection lit up the entrance to heaven. His smile was never more radiant than that morning, when he saw Juliette walking toward him down the center aisle.

As the congregation sang the final verse of the hymn, Billy Joe leaned into Juliette so she could hear him.

"Sister," he said, clasping her hand in the right hand of Christian fellowship, "are you coming to be baptised?"

She could barely speak, "Umm. No."

Not deterred, Billy Joe continued. "Are you coming to transfer your membership from another congregation?"

"No," she muttered, "I'm not."

"Then you're coming to reaffirm your faith?" asked Brother Billy Joe, beginning to run out of options.

"No, not that, either," Juliette stuttered.

"Tell me, Sister," Billy Joe asked as his smile dimmed just a little, "What can I do for you?"

Some say it was divine providence. Others call it a coincidence. But at the very moment Juliette raised her voice so Billy Joe could hear her speak, the hymn concluded and silence came over the church.

"I want to sign up for the men's breakfast and turkey shoot," she shouted, not realizing everyone could hear her.

Iris Long had made the mistake of attending the Lutheran church that fateful morning, thinking Raymond Cooper was up to something newsworthy. Who knew the events at Lennox Valley Lutheran Church would soon be overshadowed by Juliette's assault on one of the most hallowed annual events in our community?

For once, Brother Billy Joe was momentarily speechless.

Chapter Thirty-One

NOVEMBER 1998

What's Going On?

The Devil Has Everyone Talking

Monday morning conversations at the Hoffbrau were divided between questions regarding events just 20 hours earlier at First Baptist Church and discussions concerning Marvin Walsh's meeting with the Devil at Lennox Valley Lutheran Church.

Who knew, on Sunday morning as the Baptists sang "Pass Me Not, O Gentle Savior," the events about to unfold before their eyes would be anything but gentle.

Most of the news concerning Marvin Walsh was second-hand. With only 15 folks present at the Lutheran contemporary service, eye witnesses weren't easy to come by. Truth be told, even most of those present still weren't sure what had transpired.

There was even more confusion about Juliette Stoughton's outburst at First Baptist Church. While Jessie warmed up Sarah Hyden-Smith's coffee, she shared what she overheard a few minutes earlier at another table.

"I heard Vera telling Rita Tate that she was sitting in the second row, right in front of Billy Joe, when the whole thing took place."

Sarah was on the edge of her seat as she asked, "Well, what did she say happened?"

"Vera," Jessie shared hurriedly with the morning rush in full swing, "said she could clearly hear Billy Joe say, 'Sister, what can I do for you?'"

"And what did Juliette say?" asked Sarah, softly so others wouldn't hear.

117

Jessie was quick with a response. "Apparently that's when the music stopped, but Juliette didn't notice in time. Vera said she was almost shouting to be heard over the organ."

Jessie started to walk away. The Hoffbrau was packed for the morning rush, and customers were waiting.

"Wait," Sarah said. "What happened after Juliette shouted?"

Jessie leaned in as she told Sarah the last of what she knew. "Vera said Billy Joe stood there for a few seconds, almost in shock, before saying, 'Let us pray.' Apparently, while most of the heads were bowed, church deacons rushed down the aisles in record time, surrounding both Billy Joe and Juliette. The choir quickly started singing 'His Eye is on the Sparrow,' and Billy Joe, Juliette and the deacons scurried out through the choir exit."

It seemed almost like election season as most of The Valley tuned in to 880 AM to listen to "Renderings with Raymond" at noon. It seemed as if the whole Valley was buzzing about what had happened the day before and what Cooper would have to say about the events, especially since he was present at the Lutheran church when Marvin had his encounter with the Devil.

Even Iris tuned in. It was like passing by a car wreck. Everyone looks, even though they really don't want to see it. As the Monday instalment of Raymond's show began, the song "It's a Miracle" by Barry Manilow, streamed over the airwaves.

Raymond welcomed everyone to his show and bypassed most of his usual banter to allow more time for his special guest to answer calls from listeners. No one could remember Cooper ever giving up time for someone else to speak. Listeners knew there must have been something extraordinary about to happen.

"We have a very special guest with us today," Raymond began. "It's been reported that Marvin Walsh stood toe to toe with the Devil at the Lutheran church yesterday and lived to tell about it, and we're hoping that's just what he does today. Let's open the phone lines."

The first caller began to speak, "This is Essie Kennemer. I have a question for Marvin."

"What's your question?" Raymond asked.

"Marvin, what did the Devil look like? Does he really have horns and a pitchfork?"

"You know," Marvin answered deliberately, choosing his words carefully, "he doesn't look anything like that."

"Well, what does he look like, Marvin?" Essie pressed.

"The truth," Marvin responded, "is that he looks a lot like Perry Como," referring to the popular singer from the 1950s. "He was a dead ringer for Perry."

After that, the phone never stopped ringing. It was one question about the Devil after another.

"Did he try to make a deal with you? Did he smile like Perry? Did he sing that song, 'Temptation,' that Perry used to sing?"

Raymond was eating it up. Others were not as quick to promote Marvin to sainthood.

While Brother Jacob sat in his office, shaking his head and listening to the show, Frank Bell, town barber, laughed out loud as he and Sarah listened together.

Iris, sitting in her office at the newspaper, simply shook her head and muttered, "Good Lord. He's done it again."

Chapter Thirty-Two

NOVEMBER 1998

Iris's Instincts

Editor Gets to the Bottom of Sunday Events

While Raymond Cooper was giving full attention to the appearance of the Devil himself, albeit disguised as Perry Como, at the Lutheran contemporary worship service, Iris Long wasn't about to get caught up in the ensuing frenzy. Following her conversation with Jessie Orr, waitress at the Hoffbrau, during the breakfast rush, Iris turned her attention to what she felt was the most important story of the day: Juliette Stoughton's treatment by the deacons at First Baptist Church after publicly stating her desire to register for the Annual Men's Breakfast and Turkey Shoot just two weeks away.

Iris had been working on the story almost exclusively since Jessie shared Vera's version of the events which took place on Sunday morning at First Baptist Church. Unfortunately, facts were hard to come by.

The seasoned editor had confirmation Juliette went to the front of the church during the invitation hymn as the congregation sang, "Pass Me Not, O Gentle Savior." She also had confirmation that Stoughton firmly expressed her intention to sign up for the men's event. Beyond that, things got a little foggy.

Unable to reach Juliette directly, Iris left several messages on her answering machine. Remember, this was before the days of smart phones and voicemail. Iris hoped Juliette was okay and that she would eventually check her messages.

Iris's instincts told her Raymond Cooper would focus on Marvin's encounter with the Devil in his weekly rag, *The Valley Patriot.* She was convinced the devilish encounter was constructed by Cooper himself, though he would never admit to it.

Immediately after leaving the Hoffbrau that morning, Long visited Brother Billy Joe Prather at First Baptist Church. When the receptionist told Iris Brother Prather would be busy for some time, Iris said she would be happy to wait, as if she didn't have a full schedule. After a few minutes, Billy Joe made an appearance and invited Iris into his office.

Brother Billy Joe insisted he didn't have any information for the newspaper. He explained to Iris that a deacons' meeting is not a public event, and he wasn't authorized to give out any information.

Iris asked how forcing Juliette Stoughton out of the sanctuary and into some back room could be considered an official deacons' meeting, but Billy Joe held firm, eventually explaining that if she wanted information concerning the events of Sunday, she would need to speak with the chair of the board of deacons, Harley Puckett.

Harley was the younger brother of Farley Puckett, owner of Puckett's True Value Hardware. Folks in The Valley liked to joke that if Wilma Puckett would have had another son, she would have named him "Barley." Fortunately, her third child, born 10 years after Harley, was a girl, who was named "Carly," after Wilma's closest brother, Carl.

Iris left Billy Joe's office and headed straight to Puckett's Hardware, where Harley worked with his brother. As she entered the store, she was greeted by Harley.

"Good morning, Mrs. Long. How can I help you this fine morning? A lot of folks are buying grass seed today."

"I don't need any grass seed, thank you," she began. "I was hoping I could speak with you about the deacons' meeting at church Sunday morning."

"I'm not sure I understand," Harley responded. "I don't believe we held a deacons meeting on Sunday morning."

Iris got straight to the point. "I was just at Brother Prather's office to find out what happened after Juliette Stoughton was ushered out of the sanctuary yesterday. He said he was unable to tell me because he wasn't authorized to speak for the deacons."

"Oh, he did, did he? Are you sure that's what he told you?"

"Yes, I'm quite sure," answered Iris in a friendly but firm tone.

"The truth is," Harley mumbled, "I'm not sure there was an official meeting. We just wanted to be sure we understood what the young woman was saying."

"You're talking about Juliette Stoughton. That's the young woman?"

"Yes. That's her name. She seemed like a sweet girl, but we were all confused."

"Confused about what?" Iris queried.

"We were confused about why she would want to attend a turkey shoot. That's all. I mean, have you seen her? I'm pretty sure she doesn't know how to shoot a rifle."

Iris was starting to sense she wasn't going to get very far with Harley.

"You know," Harley said, "You might want to talk to Marvin Walsh. I heard he saw the Devil outside the Lutheran Church on Sunday."

"Yes, so I've heard," Iris responded, hoping she would soon be able to track down Juliette.

Chapter Thirty-Three

Deacon Digging

Iris Refuses to Give Up on Story

A less-seasoned journalist would have given up much earlier, but not Iris Long. This "was not her first rodeo," as she often said, and she had every intention of getting to the bottom of the story concerning the events at First Baptist Church on Sunday.

Juliette Stoughton had been difficult to track down, but there could have been any number of reasons for that. Maybe she was in Springfield doing a bit of shopping, or perhaps she was off meditating somewhere, as she was known to do now and then.

Iris would find out soon enough, but her primary objective was to get some solid information for her upcoming edition of *The Hometown News*. That left her just 24 hours to get to the bottom of this story before deadline.

Thinking Sarah Hyden-Smith might have an idea of Juliette's whereabouts, Iris stopped by the Methodist church just in time to hear the part-time secretary, Kari Lynn Harrell, answer a phone solicitor.

"Valley Methodist Church," Kari Lynn answered. After a pause, continued, "You'd like to speak to the owner?"

Iris knew this was going to be good. Kari Lynn had a reputation as someone who didn't waste time and especially didn't like people who wasted her time.

Kari Lynn continued. "That would be God. Should I put you straight through?"

Apparently the solicitor heard enough and hung up before getting to hear Kari Lynn's patented, "Have a holy day!"

Laughing at the "sucker" on the other end of the phone call, Kari Lynn looked up to see Iris.

"Hello, Iris," she said, still grinning. She really did like getting the best of phone solicitors. "How may I help you today?"

"I came by to see if Rev. Hyden-Smith was available," answered Iris, knowing better than to use too many words. Kari Lynn had things to do, after all.

"You just missed her," the matter-of-fact secretary answered. "She walked out of here with Juliette Stoughton about 10 minutes ago. I believe Sarah said something about walking over to the Baptist church."

"Hmmmm," Iris thought to herself. "I wonder what that's about."

"Have a holy day!" Kari Lynn shouted as Iris exited the office, quickly making her way to the Baptist church.

Iris walked up the cobblestone sidewalk leading to the Lennox Valley Baptist Church office just as her two friends were exiting. Juliette was in a frenzy about something, whispering to Sarah as fast as she could while they walked.

"Well, what a coincidence," Iris exclaimed as the two looked up to see her.

"What are you doing here?" Juliette asked.

"Well," Iris answered, "I could make something up about coming by to visit with Rev. Billy Joe, but the truth is I have been looking for you."

"Oh, I'm sorry," Juliette said sheepishly. "I've been busy, doing a lot of thinking."

"I mostly wanted to make sure you were okay," Iris offered. "I heard about your experience on Sunday, and I was concerned."

Iris wasn't trying to deceive her friend. She had been concerned, very concerned, about Juliette. Iris was a journalist, however, and wanted to know what happened after Juliette had been whisked out of the sanctuary on Sunday morning.

126

"I offered to come with Juliette to meet with Rev. Prather," Sarah said. "She wanted to speak to him, and I offered to go with her, for moral support."

"Well, do you mind telling me what happened to you after the deacons rushed you out of the sanctuary yesterday?" Iris asked. "The whole town is buzzing about it."

"They didn't hurt me or anything," Juliette answered, "but they weren't exactly nice, either. The head of the deacons, Harley some-body, told me I'd need to speak with Rev. Prather at another time. He said it was wrong for me to make a scene on Sunday."

"So you just met with him?" Iris asked.

"Yes," Juliette answered timidly.

"Well, are you going to go the Men's Breakfast and Turkey Shoot?" Long asked.

"He said I was welcome to help prepare breakfast. He said there would be a lot of nice women there. He even said I might meet a nice single man if I worked in the serving line."

Juliette turned to ask Sarah. "What do you think I should do? What would you do?"

Thinking for a moment, Sarah's face lit up. "You know. I might just have an idea." After pausing to think, she continued, "Could you both meet me at the Hoffbrau in 30 minutes?"

Walking into the newspaper office, Iris heard the last few seconds of "Renderings with Raymond" as Marvin Walsh offered his parting thoughts, "I guess the best idea is, if somebody looking like Perry Como comes knocking at your door, slam it as hard as you can, right in his face!"

Chapter Thirty-Four

Hair-Raising

Recent Events All the Talk at Local Businesses

There were a couple of businesses Valley residents frequented when they wanted to hear the latest gossip. One, of course, was the Hoffbrau. Breakfast was the busiest part of the day, and the breakfast rush was especially brisk on that Tuesday in late October.

The talk centered around two Sunday morning events. The first was Marvin Walsh's encounter with the Devil just outside Lennox Valley Lutheran Church. The second was the dramatic moment at First Baptist Church when Juliette Stoughton made a public confession: she wanted to attend the annual Men's Breakfast and Turkey Shoot.

"You know," Earl Goodman shouted, loud enough to be heard throughout the diner, "I don't think it's a coincidence that those two things happened on the same morning!"

The buzz throughout the room quieted as everyone anticipated what was to come next.

"What do you mean?" asked Kelly Schmidt, seated halfway across the room. "What does the Devil at the Lutheran church have to do with Juliette wanting to attend the turkey shoot?"

"I'm just saying," Goodman responded, "both acts were clearly the work of the Devil."

Elbert Lee Jones's voice could be heard two booths away.

"That's right," Elbert Lee muttered. "That's the gospel truth."

Just as the discussion was nearing fever pitch, Farley Puckett walked into the diner with a stack of Raymond Cooper's free rag,

129

The Valley Patriot.

There was a rush to the counter to grab copies of the free "newspaper." This was before the popularity of the Internet, and *The Valley Patriot* was The Valley's sole source of alternative news.

Iris Long didn't miss many breakfast rushes at the 'Brau. She was seated at her usual table as she watched the events of the morning unfold before her.

As she had guessed, the Patriot's lead story was about Marvin's encounter with the Devil, disguised as Perry Como. The "facts" surrounding the confrontation seemed to have come to light with increasing regularity over the previous 48 hours. Every detail was discussed and debated among the 'Brau customers.

While there was almost unanimous agreement among the 'Brau crowd that Marvin did, indeed, have an encounter with Devil, not everyone in The Valley was so quick to accept the event as fact. It just so happened that Raymond Cooper loyalists tended to find their way to the Hoffbrau early most mornings.

Just down the street at Caroline's Beauty Salon, a larger than usual group had congregated for a Tuesday morning. Most women in The Valley had their hair done on Friday afternoon or Saturday morning. At times like these, however, folks tend to go where they can find friends.

The discussion among the hair dryers was quite different from the display of emotion just down the street. Looking over *The Valley Patriot*, just after Farley Puckett dropped off 20 copies, salon patrons seemed to have a different opinion concerning the events of Sunday.

"That Raymond Cooper must think we're all idiots," offered Rhonda Goodman. "Seriously? The Devil trailing Marvin Walsh?"

"The way Marvin acts," Helen Walker jumped into the conversation, "I would think he and the Devil were already on a first-name basis."

Laughter could be heard throughout the salon. Apparently, Walsh didn't have a strong following among the hair-drying crowd.

Just two doors down, at Frank Bell's barbershop, Frank and Sarah Hyden-Smith glanced over the just-delivered newspaper.

While they both laughed at the Marvin Walsh story, what interested them the most was the weekly "A.J. Sightings" section on the bottom-right corner of the page. Apparently, in some places Elvis and Bigfoot sightings were quite normal. According to *The Valley Patriot*, A.J. sightings were beginning to become almost commonplace in The Valley.

Frank read aloud, "On Thursday, Thelma Biggers reported seeing A.J. Fryerson slipping into the office of Mayor Bland, just after sundown. She said she is sure it was Fryerson because he always wears a John Deere T-shirt and, even though it was dark, she could clearly make out the "J" on the shirt."

"Maybe it was Jesus," Frank said as he giggled at the thought of Jesus visiting the mayor's office.

"Now, Frank," rebuked Sarah. "Let's not go there."

It was then Frank turned the page to "Rumor Has It," by Maxine Miller.

"Rumor has it," Maxine began, "our Methodist pastor might be performing her own wedding before too long."

"How could she write that?" Frank muttered.

"Obviously, the Devil is working overtime in Lennox Valley this week," answered Sarah, with an audible sigh.

Chapter Thirty-Five

NOVEMBER 1998

Iris Has Gone Too Far

Marvin Walsh is Shouting Mad!

"She has gone too far this time!" Marvin Walsh shouted at Raymond Cooper as he threw a copy of *The Hometown News* across the room.

"She is a scheming, no-good, conniving she-devil," he continued. "That's exactly what she is, and I'm not standing still for it. If she wants me, she knows where to find me!"

Raymond had never seen his best friend this upset and wasn't quite sure what all the fuss was about, having not yet looked at the latest edition of *The Hometown News*.

"What has you so riled up, Marvin?" Cooper asked as he put a hand on Walsh's shoulder and guided him into a seat in front of his desk.

"She just can't leave well enough alone!" Marvin roared. "She just can't."

Raymond rifled through the 12 pages of *The Hometown News* so he could find out what had his best friend so upset.

The main story on the front page seemed to be about the upcoming men's breakfast and turkey shoot at the Baptist church. "Surely," Raymond thought to himself, "that can't be it."

"Are you upset because she didn't include your story about the Devil on the front page?" Cooper asked. "We talked about that yesterday. You knew she wasn't going to write about that. Not when her best friend is staging a one-woman protest at First Baptist Church."

"It's not that," Walsh snorted. "Look inside. Look what she wrote."

That's when Raymond found the source of Marvin's displeasure. Splashed across four columns on the top-right corner of the Opinion page was the headline:

Lutheran Disruption Seemed Like Disagreement Among Friends

"Do you see that?" Marvin yelled. "Do you see it?"

"I'm looking right at it," Raymond answered.

"Did you read what she wrote?" Walsh continued yelling. "Did you read it?"

"I'm trying, Marvin," Cooper shot back. "Just give me a minute so I can figure out what has you so riled up."

"I'll give you a minute," Walsh barked. "I'll give you a minute."

Before Raymond could get out, "Okay," Walsh was back to shouting. "Just look at what she wrote! Did you see what she said? Did you see it?"

"Simmer down, Marvin," Raymond answered, getting more annoyed with each interruption. "I see it. Let me finish reading it."

That's when Marvin grabbed the paper out of his friend's hand and started reading aloud, beginning three paragraphs into the editorial.

"'From my vantage point,'" Walsh read, "'I could see Mr. Walsh having what appeared to be a conversation with someone just outside the fellowship hall door.'"

"Of course I was having a conversation," Marvin shouted at the newspaper, "with the Devil!"

Raymond grabbed the paper back and continued reading aloud.

"'Every now and then, I could make out a bit of the conversation, although it was difficult above the sound of the worship music,'" Iris had been especially kind not to mention her real feelings about listening to the same chorus six times.

Marvin roared, "That no-good, conniving, woman editor!" before Raymond continued.

"'It almost sounded,'" Long wrote, "'like he was trying to convince someone to come into the building. My question is this: If Mr. Walsh was indeed speaking with the Devil, why would he be trying so hard to get him to come inside the Lutheran fellowship hall?'"

"Hmmm," Raymond muttered, barely audible. "What is she up to?"

"You want to know what she's up to?" Marvin shouted. "Do you want to know? Just read the rest of it!"

"'It seems to me,'" Long closed her opinion piece, "'that Raymond Cooper and Marvin Walsh were up to another one of their tricks, and if the Devil was involved, he was most likely working with them.'"

"Just what do you have to say now?" Marvin roared.

Raymond remained silent for a moment as he folded the paper back to its original format and laid it on his desk.

Neither paid any attention to the page one headline as the paper sat there:

Women's Event Provides
Alternative to Turkey Shoot

Chapter Thirty-Six

Too Funny!

Small Town News Inspires Witty Headlines

When "Renderings with Raymond" kicked off on Wednesday, Marvin Walsh was still steaming mad about the headline in *The Hometown News*:

Lutheran Disruption Seemed Like Disagreement Among Friends

At the same moment, as Iris Long sat with her friends Sarah Hyden-Smith and Juliette Stoughton over lunch at the Hoffbrau, Iris laughed about some of the humorous headlines that had graced *The Hometown News* through the years.

Both Sarah and Juliette were relatively new to the community, so they hadn't realized their older friend was such a skilled wordsmith.

Overhearing the topic of conversation, Jessie couldn't help but become involved.

"One of my favorites," Jessie said, unsuccessfully trying to hold back her laughter, "was the headline that went with the story when Melvin and Kelli Schmidt moved to town. What was that headline again?"

Iris's reticence to give an answer hinted this particular headline wasn't purposely written to be funny.

"It's slipped my mind," Iris answered, as if the words weren't forever emblazoned in her memory.

Jessie couldn't hold her laughter in any longer as she roared, "I remember now. It was 'New Residents Come From Elsewhere'!"

Both Sarah and Juliette attempted to withhold their laughter, but couldn't help but giggle a little.

"What was your favorite?" Jessie asked her friend, attempting to make up for the embarrassment she had just caused.

"I'm not sure," Iris responded. "Sometimes I just want to liven things up a bit, you know? A newspaper is more than just a source of information. It's a public service. I try to inform the public, sure. But sometimes it's fun to add a little humor to the mix."

Overhearing the conversation from his booth, Charles Marsh asked loud enough for the group to hear, "What was that headline you wrote when the poultry inspector quit his job?"

Iris laughed to herself. Obviously, she had written that particular headline on purpose.

"I believe," she said, "it was, 'Meat Head Resigns'."

Laughter erupted throughout the room as it became obvious the friends' private conversation wasn't so private. Thinking back, I'm not sure much of anything was truly private in my hometown.

"Remember the one," queried Oscar Phillips, "about the little girl's stuffed animal getting stuck in the sewer?"

"Oh, yes," Iris answered with a laugh. "I couldn't help myself when I heard about the incident. Mary Ann Tinksersly dropped her stuffed Winnie the Pooh down the storm drain on Main Street."

"That's right," shouted Phillips. "I remember now. It was 'Sewer Blocked By Large Pooh'!"

It was then Vera Pinrod walked into the 'Brau to pick up a dozen apple fritters for the evening meeting of the Auburn Hat Society.

"What's everyone laughing about?" she asked no one in particular.

"We were remembering funny headlines in the newspaper," Charles Marsh answered.

Jessie turned to Vera and said, "You've been in The Valley all your life. What's the funniest headline you remember?"

Vera rubbed her chin as she pondered the question.

"It was about five years ago, when the youth group at the Baptist church was doing a service project at the Springfield Senior Citizens Club."

Jessie began laughing, obviously remembering the story.

"What was the headline again, Jessie? Do you remember?"

"I will never forget it," answered Jessie. "It might be my all-time favorite."

"Well, what was it?" Juliette asked.

Jessie could barely get the words out, she was laughing so hard.

Mercifully, her words eventually came out. "Students Cook & Serve Grandparents."

The diner erupted in laughter.

Unlike Marvin Walsh, the group at the Hoffbrau had an appreciation for Iris Long's headline humor.

Chapter Thirty-Seven

Marvin is Mad!

Iris Long Goes "Too Far" This Time

"You know," Marvin practically snarled into his microphone, "I'm a patient man. Wouldn't you agree, Raymond?"

Raymond grinned as he spoke into his microphone in the studio of 880 AM Radio, "I certainly would, Marvin. You are a living saint among men."

Marvin continued, "But I'm here to tell you, my patience has just about run out!"

Raymond interrupted to speak to his friend, Farley Puckett, who was manning the phone. "Do we have any callers, Farley?"

"The phone has been lighting up like a Christmas tree," answered Puckett. It was a curious thing to say, seeing there were only two small lights on the phone, representing two incoming lines.

Ever calm, Raymond spoke gently into his microphone, "Let's give Marvin a moment to calm down while we take a call. Who do we have on the line, Farley?"

"Our first caller is Essie Kennemer," Puckett answered back.

Raymond greeted Mrs. Kennemer as if she were an old friend, though they'd only met in person a few times. "What's on your mind, Essie?"

"I've got something to say and I'm going to say it!" Essie shouted into her phone. "Ever since you were cheated out of the mayor's seat in that last election, nothing has been right in this town!"

Raymond loved being the center of attention and Essie was giving him the ego boost he desired.

"Well, I'm not sure we are allowed to use such language on the radio, Essie," Cooper responded, "but I understand your anxiety. Far be it from me, however, to be a sore loser. Fair or not, Silver Tongue . . . I mean, Mayor Bland, was named winner of the election."

"Winner, Shminner!" Kennemer shot back. "Him and that woman stole that election!"

Any listener would have understood Essie was referring to Juliette Stoughton, who ran against Cooper in the mayor's race.

"I understand how you feel, Essie," Raymond answered calmly. "It was mighty peculiar that a so-called 'newcomer' to our town created such a strong alliance with the most powerful official in The Valley in such a short time. Far be it from me to throw stones, though. I'm just a simple servant of the people."

"You were robbed, pure and simple!" Marvin shouted from his seat to Raymond's left. Apparently, the calming down period wasn't working so well.

"Who is our next caller, Farley?" Raymond smiled as he asked.

"It's Earl Goodman, Raymond," Puckett replied.

"Well, let's put Earl on the air," Cooper continued. "Earl, what's on the mind of our town's most illustrious federal servant?" referring to Goodman's role as Valley postal carrier.

"I want to know what is on the alleged 'mind' of our so-called 'newspaper editor'?" Goodman shouted. It seemed to be a shouting kind of day. "First, she makes that Stoughton woman out to be some kind of hero on page one," referring to Iris Long's story about Juliette's public display at First Baptist Church. "Then," Earl continued, "she besmirches the name of one of our town's finest citizens by calling him a friend of the Devil!"

"Well, I'm sure she had her reasons," Raymond interrupted, again taking reign in his role as town peacemaker.

Marvin Walsh had stayed quiet about as long as he could stand.

"I'm going to tell you something, Raymond," Walsh shouted. "I don't know what she's up to, but that Iris Long is putting her nose where it doesn't belong. The Devil had been on my back for days, trying to keep me away from church on Sunday, and here in print, she up and calls me a liar! Look there, she called me a friend of the Devil!"

"It must have been a trying moment when you saw that headline the first time," Raymond replied. "I can see why you'd be upset."

"Essie Kennemer is right," Marvin growled. "Nothing has been right around here since Bland stole the election."

Walsh took a deep breath before continuing. "And I'll tell you this. Who does that Stoughton woman think she is? Does she really think anybody is going to show up for her breakfast? What do you think, Earl? I know your wife will be cooking breakfast for the men on Turkey Shoot Saturday, won't she?"

Farley spoke into his microphone, "There seems to be a problem with the phone. Earl's line just died."

"It's probably a conspiracy!" Walsh shouted. "She's even got the phone company against us!"

Chapter Thirty-Eight

NOVEMBER 1998

Friday the 13th

Someone is Stirring Up Trouble in The Valley

Once a year, during his Mother's Day sermon, Brother Billy Joe Prather recited the same quote, credited to his grandfather, Rev. Jim Bob Prather, Jr.

"I would rather," Billy Joe would begin, before a dramatic pause, "face 10,000 soldiers, armed to the hilt," pausing again for good measure, "than to face one woman coming in the name of the Lord."

Each year, the crowd would roar with both laughter and shouts of "Amen," as if they were hearing it for the first time. Little did Billy Joe, or his grandfather for that matter, realize just how prophetic those words would prove to be.

It was mid-November 1998 and in less than 24 hours, the men of Lennox Valley would gather to feast on sausage, bacon, eggs, pancakes, biscuits, hash brown potatoes and that wondrous creation of women's groups everywhere, congealed salad.

The annual Men's Breakfast and Turkey Shoot was a Valley highlight each November, gaining more attention than Thanksgiving most years.

Interestingly, all of Raymond Cooper's regular guests on his daily radio show were unavailable for one reason or another on Friday, November 13. Perhaps they were home cleaning their rifles, or maybe they had driven to Springfield to help their wives shop for the annual men's breakfast.

Raymond always had a guest on his show. More often than not it was Marvin Walsh or Farley Puckett, owner of the local hardware store. Brother Jacob, known for his barefoot preaching, sat in the guest's seat a few times, but lately always seemed to have a prior commitment when Cooper called.

Unable to schedule any of his regulars, Raymond decided to ask the town's newest business owner, Frank Bell, to join him on the show. Frank was hesitant at first, but couldn't resist the opportunity to spend an hour with The Valley's most visible celebrity.

After exchanging pleasantries, Cooper turned to his guest and asked, "So how is the barbering business?"

Frank was thankful to have an easy question to begin the conversation.

"It's going pretty well," Frank answered. "It was a little slow at first, but now I have several regulars, as well as new customers just about every day."

Raymond continued, "Have you been building up an appetite for the men's breakfast tomorrow? Being a newcomer, you are in for a real treat. Just about every wife at the Baptist church will be in the kitchen, cooking up more food than you've ever seen."

"I'm afraid I won't be able to make the men's breakfast," Frank answered awkwardly. "I've got other plans tomorrow."

Cooper was confused. "Well, I've seen the sign on the door of your barber shop. You don't open until 10 on Saturday mornings. The breakfast is at 7:30. Even if you can't make the turkey shoot, you've still got time for breakfast."

"Yes, I know," Frank replied, "but I've got something else I need to do."

"And even if you open at 10," Raymond continued, "no one will be getting a haircut this Saturday morning. All the men will be at the turkey shoot."

What Frank didn't want to tell Raymond was he would be busy cooking for the women at the Methodist Church while the men were having their annual feast at the Baptist church.

The phone lines were eerily quiet, especially for a Friday.

Raymond surmised everyone was busy preparing for the huge event just hours away.

With no one calling in and no other guests on the Friday show, Raymond told the audience he was going to play a song for all those hunters listening to his show.

"In honor of all the mighty men who will be turkey shooting and all the sausage they will be eating," Cooper explained, "here's 'Big Bad John' by Jimmy Dean."

While the record played, Raymond frantically pressed buttons on his studio phone, attempting to reach Marvin, Elbert Lee or Earl Goodman, all to no avail. No one was answering their phones.

Raymond filled the remaining minutes of the show's final hour with a couple of his favorite songs, "Roses for Mama" and "He Stopped Loving Her Today."

He closed by reminding his audience he would be appearing live, on air, at First Baptist Church in just 17 hours as the town's men gathered to feast on the bounty provided by the town's women.

As soon as he signed off, Raymond saw the light on the studio phone blinking. It was Marvin Walsh calling.

"Where are you?" Raymond barked. "I've been looking all over for you!"

Marvin answered breathlessly, "Never mind that. We've got trouble!"

Chapter Thirty-Nine

How Dare They?
Pandemonium Threatens Annual Event

It wasn't unusual for Marvin Walsh to be incensed about some matter of "huge" importance, but there were few times Raymond had seen his friend this distressed as he ran into the radio station lobby.

"Settle down," Raymond urged his closest ally. "What in the world has you so upset?"

Marvin paused to catch his breath.

"'Upset' isn't the word!" he roared while trying to get some air. "We've got trouble. We've got big trouble!"

"What are you talking about?" asked Raymond, who was the calm one for a change.

"Did you notice all the callers on today's show?" Marvin bellowed. "Did you notice anything different about them?"

"I noticed it was mighty quiet for a Friday show," Raymond answered. "We didn't have many callers at all. I had to listen to that barber go on for what seemed like forever about haircuts. I guess my regular audience was as bored as I was."

"Oh, it wasn't the barber keeping them away," Walsh exclaimed, finally beginning to catch his breath. "It was those women!"

"What women?" asked Raymond, obviously confused.

"That woman preacher and that lady politician. Oh, and that newspaper editor!" Marvin barked. "They're the ones who kept your callers away."

"You're going to have to calm down and explain what you're

talking about," instructed Cooper.

"They've got half the women in town signed up to attend their breakfast tomorrow," Marvin explained. "And to hear people tell it, there may not be enough women to cook breakfast before the turkey shoot tomorrow morning."

"What does that have to do with folks not calling my show?" Raymond asked.

"It has everything to do with it!" Marvin shouted, obviously exasperated at his friend's lack of understanding. "Nobody wanted to call you and have to explain that their wives weren't going to be cooking breakfast tomorrow."

"Hmm," Raymond rubbed his chin as he thought aloud, "so that's why I couldn't get hold of Farley or Elbert Lee to be on my show today."

"Now you're getting it," Marvin said knowingly. "They didn't want to explain to the entire Valley that they can't control their wives."

"That is peculiar," Raymond responded, then continued, "I'm glad there's at least one man who wears the pants in his house," obviously referring to Marvin.

Walsh stood there, looking like a little boy with his hands in his pockets and his face turned down as he stared intently at nothing in particular on the floor.

"Please tell me," Cooper beseeched his friend, "your wife will be cooking tomorrow morning."

Marvin stood almost frozen. The moment was eerily reminiscent of a recent Sunday when Brother Jacob interrupted the contemporary service at the Lutheran church to ask Walsh if he was okay.

After what seemed like an eternity, Marvin stuttered, "Yes, Ima Jean is going to cook breakfast tomorrow."

"What aren't you telling me?" Raymond asked.

"It's those women!" Marvin shouted. "It's their fault. They've got all the wives in town worked up, and now they're all saying if they're going to cook breakfast, they'll be eating it, too!"

"Are you trying to tell me," Raymond said in an accusatory tone, "that your wife and the wives of Farley and Elbert Lee are going to be at the Methodist church, not the Baptist church, having breakfast tomorrow morning?"

"Well, I wasn't really trying to tell you that," Walsh answered softly. "But I guess that's about the long and short of it."

Both men were quiet for a moment, but their silence was quickly interrupted by a frantic voice just outside the radio station office on Main Street. When they looked out the window, both men recognized Bascomb Finch, shouting to anyone within earshot.

"What is it, Bascomb?" Raymond hollered as he rushed out the door. "What has you so riled up?"

"I saw him," Bascomb rambled, trying to catch his breath. "I saw him."

"You saw who?" asked Walsh, caught up in the sudden drama. "Who did you see?"

"A.J.!" Finch shouted. "I saw A.J. Fryerson walking through the playground behind the Methodist church!"

Raymond attempted to take control of the situation. "You were probably just seeing things, Bascomb. No one has seen A.J. in months."

"Don't be telling me what I saw and didn't see," Finch responded angrily. "I know what I saw and who I saw, and it was A.J. Fryerson."

At that moment, Iris Long stepped out the door of *The Hometown News* office.

"I told you we had trouble," Marvin mumbled to Raymond.

Chapter Forty

Breakfast With A.J.

Circumstances Overshadow Annual Event

If you were to ask just about anyone in my hometown in early 1998 to describe the annual Men's Breakfast and Turkey Shoot at First Baptist Church, you would have heard words such as "exciting," "fun," or "loud." Undoubtedly, a description of "hotcakes, sausages and biscuits filling plates to their brims" would follow, along with praises for the dozens of Valley wives dutifully preparing a feast in the church kitchen.

Two events conspired to ruin any hope of the usual festive atmosphere surrounding the annual affair. If it wasn't enough that Juliette Stoughton and her "crew of troublemakers" were sponsoring a competing breakfast for Valley women just across the corner at the Methodist church, Bascomb Finch had unwittingly created an atmosphere of chaos by running down Main Street on Friday night, shouting that he had seen A.J. Fryerson walking through the playground at the Methodist Church.

Raymond Cooper noticed immediately something was amiss after arriving early to set up a remote broadcast from the Men's Breakfast. Instead of the usual 30 or so women crowded around the kitchen and working to decorate the tables, Cooper counted no more than six women hurriedly making preparations.

Any other year, the Fellowship Hall would have been packed with hungry men at 7 a.m., ready for Brother Billy Joe Prather to ask God's blessings on the food they were about to receive and the targets they would soon be filling with bullets. But here it was 6:55, and there were no more than a couple of dozen men scattered throughout the room, looking hungry and a bit bewildered.

Marvin Walsh joined Raymond as they took their seats to begin the broadcast, scheduled to start at the top of the hour. At 7 a.m. sharp, the group of hungry men had swelled to approximately 120, less than half the usual size of the annual breakfast.

"I told you we had trouble," Marvin leaned in to tell Raymond in a hushed tone. "This A.J. thing has everybody riled up."

Conspicuously absent at the breakfast was Earl Goodman. A close friend of Raymond Cooper and perhaps the most vocal Valley resident in opposition of Juliette Stoughton during the mayoral election, it seemed odd that Goodman wasn't present for his favorite event of the year.

As Brother Billy Joe approached the microphone to ask God to bless the food, everyone in the room stood. Hats were removed, and chattering stopped.

The annual breakfast was no small-time activity. The ladies served breakfast as the men remained seated at their festively decorated tables.

Raymond Cooper, happy to talk about anything other than A.J. Fryerson, described the goings-on, with a bit of embellishment, to the listening audience.

"We have an outstanding group of men on hand for this year's breakfast," Cooper began, obviously less than truthful. "What do you think about today's festivities, Marvin?"

"You're right about that," Walsh responded. "This is the favorite day of the year for a lot of men in The Valley."

Describing the food heaped on his plate, Raymond said, "I don't think there's much chance I can finish all this."

The truth is the turnout was so much lower than expected, the women in the kitchen had cooked probably twice as much food as necessary. Double servings were the norm for the day.

Cooper was the first to notice Iris Long slip in the door of the Fellowship Hall with her note pad and camera. As Long wrote something on her pad, Cooper was quick to let the studio audience know about Iris's appearance.

"You know," Raymond said to his listeners, as if speaking only to Marvin, "knowing Ms. Long, she will probably distort the truth and write something to demean the gala taking place here today."

Marvin was quick to jump in, "I wouldn't doubt that one bit. That's just the type of thing she would do."

"Annnddd," Raymond continued, "it seems like she's taking pictures at angles to make the crowd seem smaller than it is."

"I noticed the same thing," Marvin snapped back. "Next thing you know, she'll be taking a picture of the wall behind her."

It was about that time Earl Goodman finally made his way into the Fellowship Hall. Walking directly toward Raymond's table, he motioned for Raymond to come toward him, obviously wanting to talk in private, without the entire radio audience listening in.

"Where have you been, Earl?" Raymond asked in a less than friendly tone.

"I went by the Methodist church to see what those women are up to," Goodman answered.

"How many folks showed up to eat?" Cooper inquired.

"Probably a couple of hundred. And it's not just the folks that showed up to eat. It's the folks in the kitchen! There are at least 20 men in there cooking for those women. And that's not all. They're all talking about Bascomb seeing A.J. last night."

Walking over just in time to hear what Earl was saying, Marvin turned to Raymond and grunted, "I told you this was going to be trouble. I just knew it!"

Chapter Forty-One

Battle of the Sexes
Valley Gets Serious Over Song Poll

In a small town like Lennox Valley, residents find entertainment in ways that would seem foreign to someone growing up in the big city. Sure, we had clubs – like the Auburn Hat Society – and church-related events, but our entertainment wasn't limited to these activities.

As editor of *The Hometown News*, Iris Long liked to do her part. One way she did this was through her Weekly Readers' Poll.

The subjects of her polls could include just about anything. Sometimes it was something as innocent as "What is your favorite ice cream flavor?" Other weeks it was downright controversial, like the time Iris posed the question, "Do you think egg price inflation is related to the Federal Reserve System?"

This issue of *Hometown News* included more than enough serious stories. With the controversy surrounding the annual men's breakfast and turkey shoot, along with the possible appearance of A.J. Fryerson a few nights earlier, Long felt a bit of levity would be good for her fellow citizens.

On Tuesday, as she sat at her desk contemplating the topic for the weekly poll, her primary objective was to come up with a question to amuse her readers. She considered:

- What is the funniest movie you've seen this year?
- How many donuts could you eat at one sitting?
- What is your favorite in-state vacation spot?

She contemplated something about the favorite menu item at the

157

Hoffbrau, but didn't want to risk the possibility that "beer" might earn a place on the list. As the only restaurant in town serving alcohol, Iris realized it was a possibility.

Eventually, she settled on a poll question that was sure to provide amusement, as well as good memories, to many of her friends in The Valley: "What is the best love song of the past 35 years?"

Iris felt certain there would be a lot of votes for "Unchained Melody," by the Righteous Brothers, and "When a Man Loves a Woman," by Percy Sledge. What she didn't expect was any controversy arising out of her innocent poll question. One would think, by October 1998, she would have known better.

You may be surprised to learn it's sometimes difficult to find exciting stories to fill the pages of a small town newspaper each week. This week was an exception. Iris had a difficult time determining which would be the main story on page 1. It would be hard to discount the possible sighting of A.J. Fryerson the previous Friday night. However, the controversy surrounding Saturday's competing breakfasts directly affected a good portion of the population.

When the paper came out on Wednesday, the front page was divided in half with a thick, 3-point line running the entire length of the broadsheet page. The A.J. story filled the left half of the page. A story about the competing breakfasts filled most of the right half of the page. The only front page item, other than these stories, was a small box underneath the breakfast story with the headline, "Weekly Readers' Poll."

The Internet hadn't made a huge dent in The Valley by 1998, so Iris collected responses to the poll in a box at the reception desk of *The Hometown News.* Folks would drop by at their leisure - deadline was noon on Monday - and leave their responses.

By Friday, Caroline's Salon was buzzing with hair dryers and chatter as Valley women prepared to look their best for Sunday services. For weeks, A.J. Fryerson had been a primary topic of discussion, but the story of his possible appearance took a back seat to the Weekly Readers' Poll.

After much discussion, it was decided that everyone present, other than Ellie Jarrell, who had already placed her vote in Iris's box, would cast their ballots for "I Never Promised You a Rose Garden," an almost 30-year-old song by Lynn Anderson.

Earl Goodman stirred those assembled at the VFW hall later that evening, when he shared that the women of The Valley were conspiring to fix the weekly poll by selecting a "feminist" song with the theme "men don't try hard enough."

Frankly, only a handful of members remembered the song from 1970, but it didn't take much to get tempers flaring in my hometown in 1998. After two hours of heated debate, the assembly agreed to cast all of their ballots for Tammy Wynette's "Stand By Your Man."

Never mind the song, recorded in 1968, was really about over-looking men's faults, the men of the VFW were giddy with excite-ment, thinking the song held the perfect message for the women who were trying to "fix" the weekly poll.

It was common knowledge Iris kept office hours on Saturday morning from 9 a.m. until noon. As she worked on the paper, she was surprised, pleasantly at first, by the number of townfolk stopping by to drop their votes into the poll ballot box.

At 12:05, Long locked the front door, sat in her chair and peeked at a few ballots. She quickly realized what was happening as almost every slip had either "Stand By Your Man" or "I Never Promised You a Rose Garden" written on it.

Leaning back in her weathered leather seat, Iris sighed, then whispered, "Oh, brother. I've done it again."

Chapter Forty-Two

Farley's List

1998 Takes Its Toll on Valley Residents

Passing through Lennox Valley, any visitor might think of my hometown as a peaceful, tranquil place during the fall of 1998. It wouldn't take long, however, to learn that life in The Valley was anything but tranquil in November of that fateful year.

Don't get me wrong. The year 1998 had its share of high points. Celebrity appearances became almost commonplace. Between TV evangelist Todd Cecil and singing superstar Tangi Blevins, there was a lot of excitement in the air.

I'm certain no one in attendance has forgotten the appearance by wrestling legend "Cowboy" Bob Orton, who lost to Jimmy Snuka after interference by Snuka's manager, Lou Albano, at the VFW post in February 1998.

Still there we were, just three days away from Thanksgiving with so much to be thankful for, yet Raymond Cooper somehow found a way to convince his listeners that times had never been worse for the Good Folks of Lennox Valley.

Hinting at tomorrow's headline in his now bimonthly newspaper, *The Valley Patriot*, Cooper spent a good deal of airtime on Monday talking about all that was wrong in The Valley. To hear him tell the story, 1998 was undoubtedly the most dreadful year in Valley history.

"I don't know about you, Farley," Raymond said to his guest co-host, Farley Puckett, owner of Puckett's True Valley Hardware Store, "but I'm not sure this town can take much more."

Puckett, long-time friend of Cooper and sole paying advertiser in

The Valley Patriot, was quick to respond.

"I couldn't agree more!" Puckett shouted into his microphone. "The events of this past weekend pretty much sum up everything that has happened to our community this year."

Puckett recited a list of "Valley disasters of 1998," which he read from the back of an envelope he had picked up at the Best Western Motel in Branson, Missouri, during a family vacation in 1976. Cooper started to ask where the yellowed envelope came from, but decided not to interfere while Farley was on a roll.

"It's like a 'Who's Who' of everything that could go wrong, and it all took place in one year!" Puckett shouted.

"You've done a lot of serious research," Cooper interrupted, obviously stroking the ego of his guest.

"You bet I have," Puckett nodded before continuing. "About the only good thing that happened this year was Dale Earnhardt winning the Daytona 500 in February. After that, the whole year pretty much went on a downhill slide."

"It was one heck of a year," Raymond chimed in, almost as if rehearsed.

"First, the Methodists decide to get a woman preacher, then a woman decides to run against you for mayor, then those two get together to try to ruin the most sacred annual event in our town."

Raymond jumped in, "You're talking, of course, about the men's breakfast at the Baptist church."

"You're darned tootin', I am," Puckett shot back before stopping to apologize to the listening audience for using such offensive language.

"So," said Raymond, taking command of the conversation, "what you're saying is that just about all of the problems in our beloved Valley this year have been caused by the so-called 'newspaper editor,' Iris Long, and her minions."

"That's right!" Puckett answered. "And I'll tell you something else. She's at it again."

"What do you mean?" Cooper asked, sounding as innocent as possible.

"I mean," Puckett shot back, "now she's making up this whole 'A.J. sighting' story to get people all worked up so they will forget everything she has done this year."

"So you don't believe that was A.J. walking through the Methodist playground 10 days ago?"

Farley was quick to answer. "No, I don't. As a matter of fact, I was talking to Barry Jarrell the other day, and he told me he took a stroll through that very playground on that very evening. I'd bet money it was Barry, alright. That Bascomb Finch had probably started his Friday night drinking early when he said it was A.J. that he saw." After pausing to let the idea sink in among listeners, Farley continued, "And that newspaper editor and preacher woman are getting half the town all stirred up believing it was A.J."

At Frank's Barber Shop, Frank Bell and Sarah Hyden-Smith were sharing a boxed lunch from the Hoffbrau and listening to Farley's rant on the radio.

Looking at Sarah, Frank spoke, "How can you be so calm when that loud-mouth is talking about you that way?"

"Let him talk," Sarah answered as she smiled. "He's just digging a deeper hole for himself."

"What are you talking about?" her friend asked. "What hole?"

Sarah answered, "Let's just say we've got a little surprise for Raymond Cooper and Farley Puckett." After a short pause, she added, "Yes, a very nice surprise."

Chapter Forty-Three

Sarah's Secret
What Does She Know That She's Not Telling?

One thing was certain about the place I grew up: The ministers who served our community were respected and admired by just about everyone.

Most, like Brother Billy Joe Prather and Father O'Reilly, had been in The Valley for some time and were greatly appreciated not only by their congregations, but others as well. While news of church scandal in other places was almost commonplace on network news, the clergy leadership of our town was something of which we could be proud.

Even newer clergypersons were welcomed with open arms. Following his Psalm 50:9 fiasco early in his preaching career, Brother Jacob seemed to find his footing and was soon well loved by most folks throughout the area. For a while, it seemed as if he might become too closely associated with Raymond Cooper, but he soon realized his time was better spent shepherding his flock instead of appearing as guest on "Renderings with Raymond."

After two years, folks still wondered why he preached in his bare feet, but after the novelty wore off, we all came to accept it without much fanfare.

Sarah Hyden-Smith had a rocky welcome, not due to anything she had done. She just happened to arrive when The Valley was overcome with fear of the Federal Reserve System. Getting their cues from none other than Raymond Cooper himself, Valley residents were wary of any outsiders, wondering if they might be in collusion with the federal government.

Eventually, however, Sarah overcame any early misgivings concerning her loyalties and was warmly embraced by most of the community. Sure, there would always be a few who were uncomfortable with The Valley's first female clergyperson, but even most of those had come to accept the Methodist pastor as a valuable member of the community.

Congregations see their clergy in various ways. The most obvious is as the preacher, the person who espouses lessons and theology in a way to bring them closer to God and each other. The aged or infirm might see their pastor as the comforter who visits when they are home-bound or in the hospital.

For some, the pastor takes on a less obvious role. It's a role they don't speak of often, if ever, during sermons. It's a commitment they often see as one of their most sacred – that of counselor and trusted confidante.

During his brief courtship of Sarah Hyden-Smith, Frank Bell had come to learn a few things concerning the life of a pastor. He learned that privacy is almost nonexistent. The good folks of The Valley sometimes knew what was going on in Sarah's life before she did. Between the weekly newspaper column, "Rumor Has It," and the ranting of Raymond Cooper each weekday from noon until 3 p.m., Sarah felt like others had the scoop on her private life before she did.

Frank had also learned there were things of which Sarah didn't speak. She sometimes had to leave suddenly to meet with "someone." He knew this meant she had a counseling appointment with a parishioner.

Sarah was, as were other clerical leaders in The Valley, a trusted confidante. She would never divulge that she was meeting with someone to discuss private matters. So when Sarah mentioned she had a little surprise for Raymond Cooper and Farley Puckett, Frank took notice.

She was hiding something, but the barber knew better than to ask what it was. What did she know about Cooper and Puckett? Or was it A.J. Fryerson she knew something about?

The possibilities were endless, but Sarah knew something, and Frank sensed a little glee in the tone of her voice when she said, "He's just digging a deeper hole for himself."

Cooper and Puckett continued their on-air conversation about Barry Jarrell and A.J. Fryerson until the top of the hour, when Sarah went back to the church and Frank re-opened his shop. Just before the 1 p.m. commercial break, Raymond shared a word of warning to his listening audience.

"You know," Cooper began, "there are those who live to stir up trouble."

Puckett jumped in, almost on cue, "You're right about that Raymond. There surely are."

"And," Cooper continued, "they will say anything to gain attention, even if what they are saying has no basis in fact."

"Preach on, Raymond!" Puckett shouted.

Raymond was on a roll as he continued. "Now I'm not saying Barry Jarrell is a bad person or that others who say they 'might have' seen A.J. Fryerson in some mysterious vehicle or walking through some park are lying."

Puckett interrupted, "Then what are you saying?"

"I'm just saying," Cooper continued, "there have been a lot of folks creating hysteria about this whole A.J. Fryerson disappearance."

Interestingly, Raymond seemed to miss, or simply ignore, the truth that most of the hysteria creation came straight from Cooper himself.

"I just want," he continued his thought, "to be a sea of tranquility in this storm of misinformation."

As he turned off the radio, Frank Bell thought he heard Sarah giggle.

Chapter Forty-Four

Iris Long is Up to Something

Raymond Cooper "Feels it in His Bones"

Like many small towns, Lennox Valley marked seasons of
the year with special events. The county fair marked the end of
summer in my hometown, while the annual turkey shoot served as a
reminder that winter chills would soon fill the air.

Thanksgiving was traditionally a quiet day for Valley residents,
when families joined together to thank their Creator for the "joyous
bounty" that had been bestowed upon them. As a child, I was never
quite sure what a "joyous bounty" was, but I wasn't about to miss out
on the turkey and all the trimmings accompanying it.

It's normal to look back on our youth as a simpler time, but
Lennox Valley was anything but simple in 1998. True, the hysteria
surrounding "Black Friday" had not reached the epic proportions
the annual shopping extravaganza enjoys today, but there was no
guarantee any day would be tranquil that year in our town.

Hometown News editor Iris Long was known to bring a chuckle
or two with her headlines now and then. In 1998, readers were
still laughing about her Thanksgiving 1994 issue. Traditionally,
the Thanksgiving newspaper was the biggest of the year, filled
with advertising related to sales which ushered in the holiday
shopping season.

Iris worked even longer hours than usual to prepare the
annual issue, which included pictures of elementary school children dressed as pilgrims, providing recipes and reminders of the
upcoming Christmas parade.

So it was in 1994 when Iris, concerned after seeing a story on

169

Nightline about the stress animals feel during the holidays, wrote a short story meant to help families prepare their pets for upcoming celebrations.

Her headline, "Preparing Pets for Thanksgiving," still adorns refrigerator doors and bulletin boards throughout The Valley. To this day, no one is sure whether the headline was a mistake or an inside joke.

On Thursday, Sarah Hyden-Smith hosted a Thanksgiving meal for a few friends who didn't have nearby family members. Sarah cooked the turkey, while Iris Long brought homemade pumpkin pie and deviled eggs.

Everyone loved Iris's pumpkin pie. Until 1992, her pie won the blue ribbon at the county fair 10 years in a row. She finally made the decision to give someone else a chance to win the ribbon.

Juliette Stoughton arrived with sweet potatoes and green beans, while Frank Bell provided homemade rolls as well as cranberry sauce purchased on Wednesday from Perry Pratt at the general store.

Following a prayer of thanks by Sarah, conversation revolved around the usual Thanksgiving topics.

"Your sweet potatoes are wonderful," Sarah told Juliette.

"How on earth do you make such good deviled eggs?" Juliette asked Iris.

"This may be the best turkey I've ever tasted," Frank offered.

It was the closest thing to a family meal these four would have, and truth be told, the three women had become as close as family. Frank and Sarah seemed to be growing closer with time, and if Maxine Miller's "Rumor Has It" could be trusted, it wouldn't be long before Frank became an official member of the family.

Across town, there was another gathering. Farley Puckett, owner of Puckett's True Value Hardware, and his wife, Martha, were hosts to Raymond Cooper and the Walsh family, Marvin and Loraine. As you might imagine, their conversation carried a different tone.

"You know, I saw that so-called 'newspaper editor' going in that woman preacher's house on my way over here," Marvin blurted out while scooping mashed potatoes.

Farley was quick to jump in, "That's interesting, because when I was at Perry's store yesterday, I heard that Stoughton woman telling Perry she was going to be at that preacher's house today."

"They're up to something," Raymond snarled. "I don't know what it is, but they're up to something, and I don't like it."

Loraine wasn't so sure. "I don't know why you say that. You always think they're up to something. They're probably just enjoying Thanksgiving together. There's nothing wrong with that."

"You women are so quick to be fooled!" Marvin shouted. "Anybody with eyes can tell they're up to something. They're always up to something."

"I heard," Farley added, "Iris Long has been going around asking people about A.J. Fryerson. She won't leave that wild goose chase alone."

"Boys," Cooper interrupted, "I believe we'd better have a special edition of 'Renderings with Raymond' tomorrow."

"What are you thinking about?" Walsh prodded.

"Don't worry about that," Raymond answered. "I know just how to handle these women."

Chapter Forty-Five

NOVEMBER 1998

The Plot Thickens

Raymond Attempts to Beat Editor to the Story

How anything so simple as a Thanksgiving dinner could be blown so far out of proportion is beyond me. That's saying a lot, since I grew up in a place where everything seemed to be blown out of proportion in 1998.

It all began when Marvin Walsh stopped by the Hoffbrau to pick up a "to go" cup of coffee – two creams, no sugar – as he did on mornings when he left home before his wife, Loraine, had time to make his morning meal.

There was no time to waste. At least not that day. Walsh was a man on a mission, or so it seemed.

His original reason for leaving home so early was to meet with Raymond Cooper and Elbert Lee Jones to make plans for the special edition of "Renderings with Raymond" taking place four hours later, at noon. Farley Puckett would meet them later in the morning, but needed to open his hardware store at 9 a.m.

Walsh's heart stopped when he saw newspaper editor Iris Long, Methodist minister Sarah Hyden-Smith, and former politician Juliette Stoughton together in the corner booth overlooking Main Street. Jessie, Hoffbrau waitress, seemed to be taking her sweet time as she poured their coffee.

"They're up to something," Marvin thought, and he was right.

As hard as he tried, he couldn't make out their conversation from the counter. He would have gone over and sat at a nearby booth, but all booths were filled with farmers, housewives, and a couple of traveling salesmen. Brother Billy Joe Prather, pastor at First Baptist

Church, walked in after Marvin. As Billy Joe talked about the beautiful morning and blessed day ahead, Walsh become especially irritated, as the chatter made it even more difficult to overhear what was being discussed in the corner booth.

When Jessie finally returned to the counter and handed Marvin his coffee which had been carefully poured into a 12-ounce Styrofoam cup, she muttered "Have a nice day" as Marvin hurried out of the diner.

She laughed to herself, sensing Walsh was irritated at something, which, after knowing him more than 40 years, she knew to be his usual disposition.

Heading straight toward the radio station in his bib overalls, Marvin was in no mood to be delayed as Helen Walker shouted, "Hello, Marvin!" from across Main Street as he approached the front door.

"I told you, Raymond," he shouted as he entered the station lobby.

"What are you yelling about so early in the morning?" Cooper asked as Walsh rushed into the studio without waiting for an invitation.

"I told you yesterday that those women were up to something, and I just got proof!"

Raymond asked, "What kind of proof? What are you talking about?"

"They're over at the 'Brau right now. I saw them with my own two eyes. That newspaper editor, that woman preacher, and that Stoughton woman are all together. I'm pretty sure Jessie is in on it, too."

"Well, it sounds like you were right," Cooper said, knowing Walsh – who still saw Raymond as his hero, even after the Federal Reserve and election fiascoes – would appreciate the confirmation.

"What are we going to do?" Marvin asked, a bit calmer.

"Elbert Lee will be here soon," Cooper began, "and we need to get Farley over here as soon as he gets things settled at his store. There is strength in numbers."

"Good thinking," Walsh replied, as if Raymond was looking for confirmation.

There was something about Raymond Cooper most of us didn't realize before 1998. He didn't seem to need anyone's confirmation. He seemed to feel invincible. Sure, he had lost the mayor's election, but that was a fluke in his mind. And his newspaper wasn't doing well. The latest issue was two weeks earlier, but he blamed that on his schedule.

"People need me more than once a week!" he'd shout into his microphone, referring to the original weekly schedule of *The Valley Patriot*. "I feel it's my civic duty to be here with you every day!" making another reference to his daily radio show.

Just then, Elbert Lee walked into the studio.

"Elbert Lee," Raymond shouted, "go find Bascomb Finch!"

"What am I supposed to do when I find him?" Elbert Lee asked innocently.

"Tell him to meet you at the Hoffbrau for lunch. Marvin and I will begin the program without you. And tell him he's going to be on my show at 1 o'clock."

"Why am I taking Bascomb Finch to lunch?" Elbert Lee asked, rubbing the top of his head.

"Don't worry about that," Cooper answered. "Just take him to lunch, and buy him at least two beers. Have you got that? Three, if you can."

Jones was confused. "Why would he drink three beers at lunch?"

"Don't you worry about that," Raymond answered. "Three beers, then bring him over to the station."

Chapter Forty-Six

DECEMBER 1998

The "Real" Truth

Bascomb Finch Clears the Air

Elbert Lee Jones dutifully did as instructed by Raymond Cooper, but that didn't mean he was pleased about the situation. "Why is it," he wondered, "I always get stuck with the dirty work?"

Let's face it. If Raymond had an important task to get done, he would assign it to Marvin Walsh or Farley Puckett. Even postman Earl Goodman, the town's only federal employee, was higher on the pecking list than Elbert Lee.

"Sure," Elbert Lee, one of two primary dairy farmers in the area, thought, "if Raymond wants eggs prices to go up a nickel, he calls me. Or if he needs something or someone hidden for a while, I'm the guy. But it's always Marvin or Farley on his radio show."

This particular assignment took the cake, as far as Jones was concerned. "Why on earth," he pondered, "does Raymond want me to take Bascomb Finch to lunch and – on top of that – buy him a few beers?"

It didn't make sense. Nonetheless, Elbert Lee did as instructed and found Bascomb at Levitt's Oil, where he pumped gas among other duties.

"Bascomb," Elbert Lee shouted as he entered the glass door, "you need to find someone to cover the gas pumps for a while today."

"What in the world are you talking about?" Finch asked innocently.

"Raymond wants you on his show today," Elbert answered. "And to show his appreciation, he wants me to buy your lunch."

Bascomb wasn't the type to get much attention, outside of his recent "sighting" of A.J. Fryerson, so an invitation to be on "Renderings With Raymond" was quite the surprise.

"Really? He wants me on his show?" Finch stood a little straighter as he contemplated the idea. "Why does he want me on his show?"

Elbert Lee Jones was getting a little impatient. "I don't know, Bascomb. Maybe he wants to brag about how you uncovered the A.J. Fryerson story. After all, you've been the talk of the town for weeks."

While not necessarily true, it was enough of an ego stroke to get Bascomb to lower his guard.

"I'll meet you at the Hoffbrau at noon," Jones told Bascomb. "We can have lunch, then walk over to the radio station. Raymond wants us there at one o'clock sharp."

When Elbert Lee returned to the radio station, he noticed Cooper and Walsh had been joined by Farley Puckett, who had just arrived after opening his hardware store. There was no time for pleasantries.

"Did you get it done?" Raymond snapped at Elbert Lee. "Is Bascomb meeting you for lunch?"

"He's coming. He's coming," Jones shot back. "Where's the fire anyway?"

"I'll tell you where the fire is!" Marvin, Elbert Lee's best friend since high school, shouted. "If you don't get Bascomb to lunch and get a few beers down him, this whole A.J. situation could blow up in our faces!"

While Raymond and crew held their "high level" meeting at the station, Iris and her "co-conspirators," as Raymond called them, were still busily talking at the Hoffbrau.

"We can hold it in the fellowship hall of my church," Sarah told her friends.

"That would be okay," Iris replied, "but it might be better if we could get the town hall, to give it the appearance of a community-wide event."

Jessie offered, "I can get the food catered by the 'Brau. We'll do it at our cost."

Back at the station, Raymond plotted with his allies, "We have to put out an issue of *The Patriot* next week."

The Valley Patriot, Cooper's once-weekly rag, hadn't been on a regular schedule for a while.

"Farley, I'll need a full page ad from you, so it doesn't look like a last-minute deal. We can use one of your old ones and change the date on it if we need to."

Farley asked the obvious question. "What are you going to write about? We don't know what those women are up to. Are you going to make something up?"

"Don't you worry about that," Raymond quipped. "We will have plenty to write about after today's show. Plus," he added, "we have the whole weekend to come up with other stories."

When high noon came, Bascomb Finch walked into the Hoffbrau and saw Elbert Lee waiting in the same corner booth previously occupied by Iris Long, Sarah Hyden-Smith and Juliette Stoughton.

"What can I get you to drink?" Jessie asked, surprised at the pair in front of her. She couldn't ever remember seeing those two together.

"I'll have a Coke," Finch replied.

"No, you won't," Elbert Lee interrupted. "You'll have a beer."

Bascomb was confused. "But it's just noon, and I have to go back to work later."

"You're having a beer," Jones insisted. "Raymond wants to thank you properly."

Chapter Forty-Seven

Tongue Twisted

Raymond Pries the "Truth" Out of Bascomb Finch

It was a strange assignment, but like any good soldier, Elbert Lee Jones carried out his duties as ordered. When Raymond Cooper ordered Elbert Lee to make sure Bascomb Finch had at least two beers with his lunch, Jones wondered why he would make such a request. Without hesitation, however, Elbert Lee had headed directly to the Sinclair station where Bascomb pumped gas.

Sitting in the Hoffbrau as Finch drank the last of his second Bud Lite, Elbert Lee wondered what Raymond was up to this time. As much as he loved Cooper, Jones knew he wasn't faultless. Raymond's scheme to raise egg prices, placing the blame on the Federal Reserve, landed Elbert Lee and his best friend, Marvin Walsh, right on the front page of *The Hometown News*. Jones didn't want to live through that kind of notoriety again.

Bascomb didn't want a beer with his lunch in the first place, and getting him to drink a second was more difficult than Elbert Lee anticipated. Eventually, Finch finished his drink and Elbert Lee paid the bill. There was no time to socialize. Raymond Cooper expected Jones to bring Bascomb into the studio of Talk Radio 880 at exactly 1:00.

Two beers didn't have much effect on Finch, as he was known to drink quite a bit more than two on occasion. Still, he was in a jovial mood as Elbert Lee led him into Raymond's studio. After all, Bascomb assumed he was going to be praised for seeing A.J. Fryerson sneaking across the Methodist church playground on that fateful night two weeks prior, and he figured Raymond would be discussing his theories about A.J.'s current whereabouts.

Cooper welcomed Bascomb into his studio and directed him to his seat. Finch had never been in a radio studio before and felt like a celebrity as he took a seat in the metal folding chair.

"Welcome back," Cooper roared into the microphone following the commercial for Farley Puckett's True Value Hardware. "Let me tell you," he continued, "we've got quite the surprise in store for our listening audience."

Bascomb's chest swelled with pride as he listened to Cooper's announcement.

Pausing just a moment for drama, Raymond continued. "We have none other than the eyewitness himself, Bascomb Finch, with us live in our studio. I'm sure, like me, you want to get to the bottom of this whole A.J. Fryerson fiasco, er, story."

Marvin Walsh, seated in a second folding chair, didn't hesitate. Almost as if rehearsed, he shouted, "I know I do, Raymond!"

Cooper turned his attention to Finch. "Bascomb," he began, "did you get to have lunch before coming over?"

"I sure did," Finch answered. "I had the Friday special over at the 'Brau."

"Oh," Raymond was quick to respond, "that catfish is pretty tasty."

"It sure enough was," Finch answered, as if he and Raymond were old friends sitting on the front porch.

"So tell me," Raymond continued, "did you have some of Jessie's lemonade with your catfish? I sure do love her lemonade."

"I can't say that I did," Bascomb responded, a little less enthusiastically.

"I guess you must have had a glass of her ice tea," Raymond quizzed further.

"No, I didn't have tea, either," Finch answered, almost mumbling.

"You seem to be a little tongue tied," Raymond pressed. "Well,

182

what did you have to drink with your catfish?"

"I was going to have the lemonade, but," Finch never got to finish his response.

"We could sit here and 'but' all day, Bascomb!" said Raymond in a louder voice. "Just tell us. What did you have to drink at lunch?"

"I had a Bud Lite," Finch answered, almost in a whisper.

"Just one?" Raymond shot back.

"Two," Bascomb replied, barely audible.

Raymond gave the answer a moment to set in as his audience hung on every word, then almost shouted, "You mean to tell me you had not one, but two, beers at lunch today?"

"You don't understand," Bascomb tried to explain, "I didn't plan to drink beer with my lunch today, but –"

"That never is the plan, is it, Bascomb?" Before Finch had the chance to respond, Raymond posed another question. "Let me ask you something. How many beers did you have that night you allegedly saw A.J. crossing the Methodist playground? Two? Six? Did you finish a 12-pack before going out that evening?"

Bascomb attempted to answer, but couldn't get the words out. As soon as he was about to speak, Cooper interrupted again.

"I think we all know the truth about what happened that night, Bascomb. I'm sure carrying this burden for these weeks has been overwhelming." Raymond was on a roll. "Well, you can relax, Bascomb. You've come forward with the truth, and my Good Book says, 'The truth shall set you free.'"

Back at the newspaper office, Iris Long sat alone, listening to Raymond's broadcast.

"Good Lord," Iris whispered to herself, "I have finally heard it all."

Chapter Forty-Eight

DECEMBER 1998

Dueling Publishers!

Cooper and Long Wage War of Words

A week had passed since Bascomb Finch made his ill-fated appearance on Raymond Cooper's radio show, but the story of his "drunken display" was still the talk of the town, thanks to Raymond Cooper and Iris Long.

The "Special Edition" of Raymond's *Valley Patriot* had filled racks around the downtown area at 9 a.m. Tuesday morning. Iris thought it was interesting to call the issue "special" since *The Patriot* advertised itself as a weekly newspaper. Just like a lot of Cooper's shenanigans, it was unusual for the paper to follow any regular schedule. He was lucky to get a new issue out twice a month.

As usual, Cooper didn't hold back any of his feelings. The headline on the front page alone was almost enough to tell his version of the A.J. Fryerson story:

A.J. Story Falls Apart as Lone Witness
Admits to Drinking Problem

Iris Long felt sure, rightly so, Cooper had cooked up the entire "drunken Bascomb" story, but as usual, Raymond had his listeners and readers eating out of the palm of his hand.

Raymond was certain he had put the Fryerson story to rest, once and for all. His live interview with the sole witness to the lone alleged appearance of A.J. Fryerson put the matter to rest for good, as far as Cooper was concerned. What he didn't realize, however, was Iris Long had something up her sleeve, as well. Being a jour-

185

nalist for five decades had created a sixth sense in Iris. She knew to cross every "t" and dot every "i." She also knew to be ready for any surprise that might come her way.

Raymond wasn't as educated as Iris in the ways of print journalism. While Long followed all the traditional journalistic standards, Cooper flew by the seat of his pants. Iris would never print a story without a minimum of two sources. Cooper saw sources as an obstacle and often ran stories that were no more than his own version of reality. Nonetheless, his readers and listeners hung on Cooper's every word, believing them to be inspired by someone, or something, greater than Raymond himself.

When Long's *Hometown News* arrived in town Wednesday morning, it was as if a natural disaster of some type had struck.

Marvin Walsh and Farley Puckett were sitting in a booth at the Hoffbrau at 9:42 a.m. when Barry Jarrell arrived with a stack of *Hometown News* copies under his arm. Before he could hand the newspapers to Jessie, patrons rushed to get their own copies, dropping quarters by the cash register as they hurried back to their booths.

Raymond Cooper had dropped the gauntlet. Every citizen in The Valley was on pins and needles to read how Iris would respond.

Along with the community calendar down the left sidebar, there were two stories on the front page of *The Hometown News*. Beneath the fold – that's the bottom half of the page – was a story almost no one noticed on Wednesday morning.

The headline under the fold read:

Methodist Church to Host New Year's Eve Party: Everyone Welcome.

It was interesting that Iris would place such a nondescript story on the front page. There must have been more to the New Year's Eve party than met the eye.

No, it wasn't the special event at the Methodist church everyone noticed. It was the headline, in 80 point type, spanning across five columns at the top of the page:

Final Letter From A.J. Fryerson Foretold
His Disappearance From Valley

You could have heard a pin drop as 'Brau patrons read those words, then followed with their eyes to the story below. Two, sometimes three, readers crowded around copies of *The Hometown News* in every booth.

As readers followed the story from the front page to the "jump" on page 8, Marvin Walsh and Farley Puckett hurried out of their booth and made a hasty exit from the diner.

It took most folks a while before reading the story about the upcoming party at the Methodist church. But when folks finally got around to that story, they noticed another valuable piece of information they could have easily missed in the excitement over the A.J. revelation.

Raymond was perhaps the only resident of The Valley to notice that tidbit immediately: "Rev. Sarah Hyden-Smith, pastor of Lennox Valley Methodist Church wants everyone to know a very important surprise announcement is going to take place during the party."

Looking over the page, Cooper snarled, almost to himself, "This isn't over yet."

Chapter Forty-Nine

DECEMBER 1998

Could She Know?

Holiday Joy Seems to Bypass Raymond & Friends

While much of Lennox Valley huddled around fireplaces in homes filled with families and friends after attending one of the many Christmas Eve services on the town square, Raymond Cooper, Farley Puckett, Marvin Walsh and Elbert Lee Jones gathered around the lobby of The Valley's only radio station to discuss more important topics.

After hearing Rev. Sarah Hyden-Smith promise a "special announcement" at the upcoming Valley New Years Eve party, the foursome was awash in fears of what the town's newest pastor had up her clerical sleeve.

"Do you think she knows?" Marvin Walsh asked in a worried tone.

"How could she know?" Farley Puckett shot back. "Did somebody here start flapping their mouths?"

"Everything has gone haywire since Bascomb saw A.J. in the Methodist playground," noted Marvin.

"Settle down, boys," said a calm Raymond Cooper. "Nobody believes Bascomb saw anything after he came on the show. Everybody thinks he was drunk that night."

"Well, somebody knows something!" shouted Elbert Lee.

"Now listen," Cooper continued. "We don't know that she knows anything. That announcement could be about something totally unrelated to A.J. Maybe those Methodists are building a new building or something. Methodists love to build buildings."

189

Three blocks away, Juliette Stoughton, Iris Long and Frank Bell gathered around Sarah's Christmas tree, enjoying a holiday amongst friends. After all, these four weren't acquainted just a year earlier, and now they were quite close. Well, three of them were quite close. Frank was growing increasingly close to Sarah and was now considered the lone male member of the "family."

No mention was made of Raymond Cooper. It was a time to celebrate a child born long ago in a faraway place. It was a time to celebrate new friends. True, Iris's husband, Ed, had passed away ten years earlier, and Juliette's one-time soulmate, Chris Roadhouse, was fading from memory. But there were many things for which to be thankful. Yes, there was truly something special about the year 1998.

Over on Vanosdale Drive, Earl and Rhonda Goodman shared a slice of chocolate cake covered in cherry icing. It was a tradition in their home to have dinner before Christmas Eve service, then enjoy dessert together by the warmth of their fireplace.

Elbert Lee, Marvin and Farley eventually made their ways home, all knowing their wives wouldn't be happy about spending so much of Christmas Eve alone. As they left the radio station, Raymond shouted, "Let's talk tomorrow. We have to come up with a plan."

Brother Jacob, assistant pastor at Lennox Valley Lutheran Church, was on his way to his church when he came upon the three culprits leaving Cooper's station.

With a laugh, Jacob said, "I thought I had run into three wise men for a moment."

Asking the trio if any of them would be at the midnight service at his church, all three hurried on, with Marvin muttering something about getting home to his wife.

Marvin was obviously still embarrassed about his last visit to the Lutheran church. That was the morning he had his encounter with the Devil himself, just outside the door of the Lutheran fellowship hall.

Almost all the good folks of The Valley were home. Some would wander out in a few hours to attend a midnight service at the Catholic or Lutheran church. Others would be busy helping Santa arrange presents under the tree.

There was one exception, however. As Lennox Valley folks celebrated the gift of Christmas, one Valley resident made his way to his car and headed down Highway 11 toward Springfield, the county seat.

As he passed the empty VFW post, Raymond's thoughts momentarily drifted back to the election rallies he had attended just a few months earlier. It was a time of promise, but something had gone wrong.

"I'm not going to let them get away with this," Cooper muttered under his breath. "Not this time. Not again. They have been a thorn in my flesh for too long."

Driving north on Highway 11, Father O'Reilly, on his way back to The Valley after visiting shut-ins on Christmas Eve, noticed Cooper pulling into the parking lot of the closed Phillips 66 station just inside the Springfield city limits.

Looking as closely as possible while driving down a lonely highway on a dark night, the "Good Father" noticed a thin man in overalls and a heavy coat walking toward the passenger's door of Cooper's 1994 Buick Skylark.

"I wonder what he's up to now," Father O'Reilly whispered to himself.

Chapter Fifty

New Year's Eve

Perhaps the Craziest Moment of the Craziest Year

Who knew at the beginning of the year that 1998 would be the most bizarre year in Valley history? At the time, Raymond Cooper was no more than a radio "nut job" espousing his theories about UFOs, the federal government and other outrageous topics.

In January, there was only one newspaper in town, *The Hometown News*. None of the good folks had met Juliette Stoughton, and the idea of a female minister at the Methodist church was the furthest thing from anyone's mind.

Even with everything that transpired in 1998, the most outrageous memory has to be the disappearance of the town complainer, A.J. Fryerson.

There we were, on New Year's Eve, assembled in the fellowship hall, sanctuary and Sunday school classrooms of Lennox Valley Methodist Church. Thank heavens it was warm for December, as hundreds of folks, mostly ones with young children, gathered on the church lawn and playground wearing overcoats and mittens.

I don't think anyone expected such a big crowd. Even though the story in *The Hometown News* quoted Rev. Sarah Hyden-Smith inviting everyone to come to the Methodist church for a very special announcement on New Year's Eve, no one anticipated most of The Valley would show up.

Conspicuous in their absence were Raymond Cooper and his minions. Raymond, Elbert Lee, Marvin Walsh and Farley Puckett were nowhere to be seen. Cooper's other devotee, Earl Goodman, arrived with his wife, Rhonda, early in the evening, but excused himself to visit the restroom soon after. That may have been the longest restroom visit in Valley history, because no one remembers seeing him again until just before midnight.

This was 1998, a time before huge video screens adorned the walls of churches as they do today. Perry Pratt, owner of the general store, used his connections at the junior college in Springfield to borrow a video projector, something most Valley folks had never seen, so everyone could count down the New Year with Dick Clark as the giant white ball made its way to the ground in far away Times Square, New York.

So there we were – Methodists, Baptists, Catholics and Lutherans young and old. The whole town had been talking about the New Year's Eve party since it was announced weeks earlier. It was the social event of the season in my hometown.

There was fruit punch and all types of desserts prepared by the Methodist women's group. Anyone who knows anything about Methodist women knows they sure can put out a spread of food.

Even Brother Billy was secretly envious of the spread put out by the Methodists. They always seemed to outdo the other churches when it came to cooking.

Foreseeing an obvious shortage in refreshments as the throng filled the church, Perry Pratt made a trip to his store and loaded pies, cookies and cakes into his truck. It would be his donation to the festive event. Later, 20 minutes before the shiny white ball would drop from the sky announcing the New Year, Perry decided to make a second "snack run" to appease the hungry crowd. He loaded the last of his cakes and pies into the back of his pickup truck and headed back to the church.

While Pratt was loading his truck, Sarah Hyden-Smith gathered the crowd for an announcement. As the TV volume was muted, silencing the sound of Dick Clark and a million revelers on Times Square, the crowd hushed.

"This must be it," Vera Pinrod was overheard saying to her best friend, Helen Walker. "She's going to make her announcement."

"As promised, I have some very important news to share with you," Sarah began. The crowd stayed silent. "What I would like to tell you is . . ."

At that moment, the entire church, including the lights on the church lawn and playground, went black.

"There must be a power outage," Earl Goodman shouted, back from his noticeably long bathroom visit. "I guess we should just go home."

At that moment, a commotion was heard outside. Suddenly, the lights came back on, and Chief Dibble came through the crowded fellowship hall, pulling Raymond Cooper and Marvin Walsh behind him.

"I found these two, along with Elbert Lee and Farley, out by the fuse box. Elbert Lee had a fuse from the box in his hand," snarled Dibble.

"There is a simple explanation," Cooper shouted. "We were simply putting a new fuse in the box, after seeing the lights go out from the station lobby."

Just then, Iris Long did something no one in the throng will ever forget. She made her way through the crowd, walked up to Raymond Cooper, and smacked him – hard – across his face.

"We have put up with your lies and shenanigans long enough!" Iris shouted. "You and your friends did everything you could to keep Sarah from making her announcement, and it didn't work."

Turning to face the assembly, she roared, "Who wants to hear Sarah's announcement?"

On the huge screen, made from four king-size sheets sewn together by the Baptist quilting group, on the wall directly behind Sarah, Dick Clark made his way through the crowd. He was visiting with folks who had come from all over the world to celebrate the arrival of a new year. There were Barry and Kim from Tennessee.

Michelle and Jeff Van Hee had their sleeping son, Derrik, with them.

"I'm ready to make my announcement," shouted Sarah.

The crowd grew silent. You could have heard a pin drop.

"On March 6, I will become the wife of Frank Bell!"

There were cheers from some in the crowd, while others stood in shocked disbelief.

"Wait, that's it?" roared Phil Moore.

"Yeah, what about A.J. Fryerson?" Boyd Sanders yelled.

"What do you mean?" asked Sarah. "Why would I know anything about A.J.?"

At that moment, Jessie, waitress at the Hoffbrau, screamed at the top of her lungs, "Everybody be quiet! Turn up the volume on the TV!"

I was there, and I can honestly say I have never seen anything so utterly amazing and probably never will again. For as we stood, staring at the screen as Ken Bell fiddled with the volume button, we saw the most amazing sight on the TV.

There was Dick Clark, holding his microphone up to a familiar face in the crowd, though we still couldn't hear anything. Suddenly words appeared beneath the talking figure – "A.J. Fryerson."

Finally, Ken got the volume working just in time to hear Dick Clark say, "That is the most bizarre story I have ever heard, A.J.," before turning his attention to the sky, announcing, "It's time!"

The crowd inside and outside the Methodist church joined with the crowd in Times Square and crowds gathered in hamlets and villages throughout the land as they counted:

10! 9! 8! 7! 6! 5! 4! 3! 2! 1!

Happy New Year!

I enjoyed my first New Year's kiss with MaryAnn Tankersly, the prettiest girl in Lennox Valley, at the stroke of midnight.

As far as I know, no one recorded *Dick Clark's New Year's Rockin' Eve* that night. For years, we wondered how A.J. ended up on Times Square as 1998 came to a close. Eventually, we learned what really happened to him.

But that, as they say, is another story for another day.

Made in the USA
Columbia, SC
07 October 2020